BLACK RULES

CHARLOTTE BYRD

PRAISE FOR THE BLACK EDGE SERIES

"Titillation so masterfully woven, no reader can resist its pull. A MUST-BUY!" - **Bobbi Koe**

"Captivating!" - **Crystal Jones**

"Exciting, intense, sensual" - **Rock**, Amazon reviewer

"Sexy, secretive, pulsating chemistry..." - **Mrs. K**, Amazon reviewer

"Fast-paced, dark, addictive, and compelling" - **Clpetit56**, Amazon reviewer

"Hot, steamy, and a great storyline." - **Christine Reese**

"My oh my....Charlotte has made me a fan for life." - **JJ**, Amazon reviewer

"The tension and chemistry is at five alarm level." - **Sharon**, Amazon reviewer

"Hot, sexy, intriguing journey of Elli and Mr. Aiden Black. - Robin Langelier

"Great start to fantastic series!" - **Brenda**, Amazon reviewer

"Sexy, steamy and captivating!" - **Charmaine**, Amazon reviewer

" Intrigue, lust, and great characters...what more could you ask for?!" - Dragonfly Lady

"An awesome book. Extremely entertaining, captivating and interesting sexy read. I could not put it down." - **Kim F**, Amazon reviewer

"Just the absolute best story. Everything I like to read about and more. Such a great story I will read again and again. A keeper!!" - Wendy Ballard

"It had the perfect amount of twists and turns. I instantaneously bonded with the heroine and of course Mr. Black. YUM. It's sexy, it's sassy, it's steamy. It's everything." - **Khardine Gray, Bestselling romance author**

ABOUT BLACK RULES

*W*e don't belong together.

I should have never seen him again after our first night together. But I crave him.

I'm addicted to him. **He is my dark pleasure.**

Mr. Black is Aiden. Aiden is Mr. Black. Two sides of the same person.

Aiden is kind and sweet. **Mr. Black is demanding** and rule-oriented.

When he invites me back to his yacht, I can't say no.

Another auction.

Another bid.

I'm supposed to be his. But then everything goes wrong....

PROLOGUE - AIDEN

I don't know what has come over me.

I've become obsessed with Ellie. Maybe even addicted to her. I want to see her all the time.

I want to touch her. I need her to touch me. I crave her presence. When she's not around, the hours drag by at a snail's pace.

And when she is around, my body gets filled with so much excitement, I'm practically bouncing off the walls.

She has forgiven me for taking her to the live sex club, but I haven't forgiven myself. I should've known better, but I've been so completely immersed in my own world that it didn't even occur to me that she wouldn't necessarily be into it.

The thing about my world is that women are always throwing themselves at me. I've been on the cover of Fortune and Time, and numerous gossip magazines and newspapers have started to refer to me as New York's (and by that, the world's) most eligible bachelor.

And this title comes with certain responsibilities. I need to be seen and photographed with various socialites and celebrities at least once a week. And not just photographed.

Women have expectations when they are taken on dates by eligible bachelors. They want to be wined and dined and fucked accordingly.

Well, I've known Ellie only a week, I'm already falling behind in my duties.

There hasn't been one scandal and my public relations manager is at a loss as to what to do.

I mean, she does get paid a pretty penny to keep my name clean even if I do everything in my power to dirty it up.

"I'm sort of seeing someone." I try to explain when she questions me on the phone.

"You are? Who? Is it the heiress to the Warrenhouse fortune?"

She rattles off a few other promising possibilities - women I've been linked to during the past few months.

But I keep saying no, no, no.

"So, tell me. I mean, this is huge news."

"No, it's not." I shake my head. "It's not news at all. I don't want it public. We don't want it public."

I correct the word *I* to the word *we* because I actually have no idea how Ellie would respond to any of this.

And I don't want to spring it on her. I need for things to remain as normal as possible between us because I'm terrified of breaking the spell that she has put me under.

"Listen, I can't talk about this anymore. I'm spending the weekend on the yacht again. I'll be in touch afterward."

After hanging up abruptly, my thoughts turn back to Ellie. She's actually going to the yacht party again. I thought that she would, but I wasn't completely sure.

I know that going to the last one was a big deal for her.

Very out of character.

That's one of the reasons why I like her so much. She is very much unlike all the typical girls that I tend to meet.

And I do like her.

No, that's not the right word, is it?

It's more like love.

I already told her that I'm falling for her.

But that was a lie.

A big lie.

I'm in love with her.

And I think I've been in love with her since the first night that we spent together.

I just haven't told her yet. It's too soon, right? I mean, we just met. I don't want to freak her out. I don't want to come on too strong.

And yet, this is how I feel. And I also know that I'm a

coward for not telling her the truth about my feelings.

I open the banking app on my phone.

Speaking of Ellie, I still owe her the rest of the money for the week she has agreed to be mine. The week didn't go exactly as planned, but I'm a man of my word and I always pay my debts.

Somewhere in the back of my head, I get a nagging feeling of insecurity.

What if she's only spending time with me because of the money?

I know she has never done anything like this before, but that doesn't mean that the money isn't alluring.

Enticing.

Captivating.

What if this whole thing has been a game?

What if it's just pretend?

I transfer the rest of the balance I owe her and toss my phone on the couch.

I guess this weekend I will find out for sure. I'm not paying her any more money to be with me.

So, if she continues to act just as interested and our connection remains strong, then what I'm feeling is real and authentic.

And if she doesn't?

My heart drops a bit.

I guess it has all been a charade and I'll have to pick up the broken pieces of my heart and move on with life.

What else is there to do?

Just then, my phone rings. My heart skips a beat at the thought that it might be Ellie.

But when I glance down at the screen, I see that it's Alexis.

My ex-wife.

Fuck.

I don't want to pick up, but I know her too well. She'll just keep calling.

"What do you want?"

"I just wanted to tell you that you're an asshole." She starts talking almost immediately.

This is her natural state - rushed and out of control.

Whenever you enter a conversation with her, it feels like you've been in it for quite some time and you're always playing catch up.

"What is it now?" I ask.

"I come to you for help and you just turn me away. I mean, what kind of friend does that?" she asks.

"Alexis, it's not my fault that your husband took off on you and Rory. He's an asshole. But I told you that a million times. I also told you to leave him a million times. I said I would help. But do you listen? No, of course not."

"Whatever."

I don't know what else to say.

Alexis' modus operandi is drama.

She needs constant stimulation in her life to give it meaning. I didn't understand that when we were married.

I tried to calm her down.

I tried to make peace.

But that's not what she wants.

She wants something more exciting.

And I'm just not the person to give her that anymore.

"I'm busy," I say after a moment of silence. "I have to go."

"Why can't you just be there for me? Don't I mean anything to you anymore?"

I hang up the phone. No, you don't, actually. That's what I think, but it's not something I can say out loud.

I'm not that cruel. There was a time when I was desperately in love with Alexis.

She was tall and beautiful and full of life. She's still tall and beautiful, but what I used to think was her exuberance was just a desperate attempt to fill her life with drama.

And I don't have time for that. I need my life to be calm and predictable. At least, when it comes to relationships. Well, not really relationships.

I don't really know what I need in a relationship.

The truth is that I haven't been in one since I was with Alexis, and I've used women mainly to have a good time with.

Sex.

Food.

Fun.

More sex.

That's all I've really had since Alexis.

Until I met Ellie.

CHAPTER 1 - ELLIE

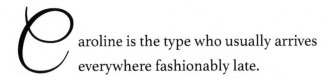aroline is the type who usually arrives everywhere fashionably late.

But not this time.

Tonight, she's rushing me.

Telling me to hurry up.

Yelling at me and only making me move slower.

Unlike other girls, I can't even shop with other people well because I need to focus on picking out clothes and that takes a lot more resources from me than other normal girls.

"What the hell is taking you so long?" Caroline stands in my doorway.

Her bag is already packed and she's wearing the dress and heels that she will be wearing out. Meanwhile, I'm still in my pajamas and slippers.

"Listen, I told you. I need to think, okay? We still have half an hour before the cab gets here."

She rolls her eyes and mouths whatever. She finds me tedious and boring.

I know that.

She wants to pre-game, meaning that she wants to do a few shots to calm her nerves.

I know she's nervous.

So am I.

But she doesn't believe me.

Even though I've been to the yacht before and participated in the auction, that doesn't mean that I know what I'm doing. She has been to the yacht before, too.

This isn't all new to her. I mean, I would never even have met Aiden if I hadn't gone to the party with her.

But something about that night made me braver

than Caroline. While she's always the one having one-night stands and going home with strange men and going away for weekends on a whim, she didn't want to be auctioned off that night.

Come to think of it, I don't really know why I actually did it except that it felt like it would be an exciting thing to do.

You see, if you live long enough as a boring, predictable sort of girl, you end up craving something different. Something fun.

You want the world to see you as someone else.

Or maybe you just want to see yourself as someone else.

It's not all the time that you actually have the ability to surprise yourself.

Fifteen minutes later, my bag is finally packed.

I take a small makeup bag with me and check my hair in the mirror. I change into a pair of skinny jeans and boots and a tight-fitting, but warm jacket, which is cut in such a way that it makes my butt look amazing.

"What the hell? You're not wearing a dress?"
Caroline asks.

She's dressed in a lacy, black number, which is
sleeveless to boot.

I shrug.

"The weather is getting colder," I say. "It's not
summer anymore."

Unlike most twenty-something girls in Manhattan,
I'm somewhat of a wimp.

These girls will wear stiletto heels and strapless
dresses in the dead of winter when it's like twenty
degrees out and snowing. They'll take a few shots to
warm up and then leave their apartments without so
much as a long sleeve shirt to keep them warm.

No, I could never do that.

Not in college, not now.

I'm cold practically all the time as it is, even when it's
not February in New York City.

And even though it's only September and the days
are still pretty warm, I'm worried that I'll be cold on
the yacht.

Besides, I look hot. Just not dressed up. Jeans and a nice-fitting top are always my go to outfit. It makes me feel safe. Not too overexposed.

"Ah, whatever. It's not like there's time to change," Caroline says, opening the door to our apartment.

She has already called the cab and it's waiting patiently for us downstairs.

"I'm so excited," Caroline whispers to me in the cab.

She never talks at full voice in cabs. I'm actually not sure which is ruder. I mean, it's not like the cab driver can't hear her even if she whispers.

He just can't hear her as well.

"Yeah, me, too."

The cab driver drops us off at the familiar nondescript office building.

It's the same place where we helicoptered out of last time and we go through the motions like experts. The security guard inside nudges us toward the elevator and tells us to head to the top floor.

This time, the roof isn't particularly windy and I can

enjoy the view a little more. New York is lit up in all directions, except for the water, which is pitch black.

The helicopter pilot helps us with our bags and hands us earphones to wear inside. Within a few moments, we are flying high above the skyline. The skyscrapers look like models now, something that a little kid would play with.

And the people below are practically non-existent. They're as small as ants.

"It's beautiful, isn't it?" Caroline asks.

"Yes!" I scream so that she can hear me.

Caroline pulls out her phone and takes a few selfies. But I decline.

I don't feel like faking a smile now.

My stomach is in knots over the anticipation of what is about to happen.

———

SINCE IT'S ALREADY dark outside, I know that we are flying over water but there is only blackness below us.

Somewhere in the distance, I see a few lights and feel the helicopter get into position.

A few minutes later, we land.

At the entrance to the main living room, a familiar face greets us.

Lizbeth, the woman who greeted us before and ran the auction. She is just as tall and beautiful as I remember. She's again holding a silver plate with glasses of champagne. The man in an impeccable tuxedo next to her helps us with our bags.

"It's nice to see you again, Ellie," Lizbeth says, showing us to our stateroom. "You will not be sharing a room this time. The rooms are right next to each other though."

Wow, we're moving up in the world, I want to say, but I keep my mouth shut.

Lizbeth shows Caroline into her room and the man in the tuxedo drops off her bag. She tries to tip him, but he refuses to accept anything.

"You are guests of Mr. Black," Lizbeth explains. "And guests of Mr. Black do not tip. Besides, everyone working on this yacht is generously compensated."

I nod, slightly relieved by this fact. I suddenly remember that I did not tip the guy last time and was already feeling bad about that.

In restaurants, I always tip twenty percent no matter what kind of service I get.

Why?

My aunt, my mom's sister, got pregnant in high school and worked as a waitress at a low-rent diner all of her life.

Unlike other places of employment, waiters are not required to be paid a minimum wage.

Employers only have to pay them $2.13 per hour because the rest of their wages are expected to come from tips. But the problem is that if the diner or restaurant isn't busy, then they usually don't make even minimum wage.

So, I always tip waitresses twenty percent, but I have no idea how much I'm supposed to tip cleaning people in hotels, and butlers, and other staff for things like turndown service and helping with bags.

It's mainly because I never really stay in places that have offered those services before.

"The cocktail party has begun. Feel free to join us when you're ready," Lizbeth says, opening the door to my room.

The man in the tuxedo drops off my bags and I let out a sigh of relief because I don't have to scramble and worry if I'm leaving him enough of a tip.

"Oh my God!" Caroline bursts into my stateroom. "How gorgeous is this place?"

I walk around my room and take it all in. It's just as beautiful as the last room we shared, but different. The fact that it's called a room is a misnomer.

It's actually a one-bedroom apartment with a large sitting/living room area and a separate bedroom. I run my fingers over the fine Egyptian linens and follow Caroline as she shows me into the bathroom and gushes over the marble his and hers vanity.

Back in the sitting room, I make note of the soft lighting that creates a mood of opulence and luxury and then go out onto my private balcony and look out onto the vastness of the ocean.

"This is amazing," I say to Caroline.

She nods excitedly, fixing her makeup.

"Shall we?" she asks, taking me by the arm.

My heart skips a beat, and I follow her out to the cocktail party.

CHAPTER 2 - ELLIE

WHEN WE GO TO ANOTHER COCKTAIL PARTY…

*W*hen we get to the main cabin on the yacht, the place is filled with young, attractive people.

The guys are in their twenties and thirties and dressed in expensive tailored suits with starched white collars and cufflinks. At the bar, I order a mojito and Caroline gets a martini.

After a few sips, my nerves calm down a bit and I relax in the swivel chair. Caroline gets busy chatting up the two hot guys positioned right next to us, but I look around the room for Aiden.

My hopes go up every time a new person enters the room, but forty minutes and two drinks later, he's still not here.

This isn't unusual, of course.

He didn't come to the cocktail party last time either. But it's still a bit of a letdown.

I haven't talked to Aiden since he insisted on me coming to the party and I am not entirely sure where we stand. He paid the rest of the balance he 'owed' for spending the week with him, even though he didn't really owe it to me.

The week didn't really go as either of us had planned, and I wouldn't have minded if he had not paid the rest. Still, he's a man of his word and my bank account grew by quite a bit as a result.

The odd thing though, is that his transferring the rest of the money to me actually brought about more questions than answers in my mind.

I mean, where do we stand now?

Will there be another auction tonight and do I sit it out?

There's no way I'm going to participate and go to the highest bidder who isn't Aiden.

But why would he want to pay for my presence

again?

Frankly, I don't really want him to. I want to be with him because he wants me and I want him, not because of any monetary exchange or requirement.

With all of these questions weighing heavily on my mind, I struggle to make conversation with the guy who is desperately trying to chat me up.

He's telling me about his time at Princeton and I simply stare into my drink and nod along, wondering how much he will be spending on a girl tonight, or if he will be participating at all.

When Caroline and the two guys she has been chatting with join our conversation, I overhear the rumors that are going on about what's going to happen on the yacht later.

"I heard that there will be a masquerade ball," one of the guys says.

"No, I think there's going to be a dinner first," the other one says.

"Well, actually, Ellie here has been to one of these before," Caroline says with a coy smile and a mischievous twinkle in her eye.

"Really? What happened?" The guys demand
to know.

I shake my head and shrug, but Caroline doesn't let
me get off that easily.

"Actually, they had an auction. Girls who were
willing were auctioned off to the highest bidder,"
Caroline says. "Hope you guys brought your
checkbooks."

That definitely leaves an impression as they start to
talk among themselves. A part of me is annoyed
with Caroline for telling them about the auction, but
another part isn't all that surprised.

Out of the corner of my eye, I spot a man by the
other side of the wall.

He's definitely easy on the eyes and even more attractive
than the rest of the hot men around here. There's a
serious brooding look on his face and he looks familiar.

Suddenly, it occurs to me that I've seen him before.
He was one of the men I talked to last time. His dark
piercing eyes stare into my soul and I can tell that he
remembers me, too.

He brushes his fingers through his dark chocolate hair and makes his way over to me. When he gets close, I lose myself in the brilliance of his eyes; they are the color of the ocean.

"Ellie, right?" he asks in his low voice.

He has a strong square jaw and an elegant nose that is a perfect fit for his face.

I search my mind for his name, but can't come up with anything.

"Blake Garrison."

He extends his hand to me.

"Oh, that's right," I say, shaking his hand and wondering how he knows my name.

We have talked before, at the last party, and his stare was just as disarming then as well.

And then it hits me!

That's right.

Of course.

He's the guy who wanted a private word with me.

He's the one who told me that I shouldn't be at
the party.

It was a warning of sorts.

A warning I still have no idea why he gave.

"Weren't you the guy who told me that I shouldn't be
here last time?" I ask, crossing my arms across
my chest.

He nods and winks.

"And why was that again?"

"Just didn't think that this sort of party was a good fit
for a girl like you," he says after a moment.

I clearly took him aback by confronting him.

"And what do you know about me?"

"You seem like a nice girl, that's it."

"Well, I am. But maybe nice girls can have a good
time, too. Besides, it's very presumptuous of you to
make that kind of statement to strangers. Don't
you think?"

Blake shrugs and orders an old fashioned. He's
ignoring me. Goading me. It's incredibly irritating.

"Well, I had a good time anyway," I say. "And that's why I came back."

"Yes, I see that."

"And clearly, you had a good time, too. Since you're back."

Blake takes a sip and shrugs nonchalantly. "I guess you could say that."

"Why else would you be back?"

"I came here for what I want. I didn't get it last time, so I'm hoping I will this time," he says, staring straight into my eyes.

The serious look on his face sends chills through me.

No, this isn't flirting or joking anymore.

Every fiber in my body says that this guy is trouble and I need to stay away.

Luckily, the cocktail hour quickly comes to a close and Lizbeth disperses everyone to their own rooms.

————

Somewhat familiar with the process, I join Caroline in her room.

Lizbeth is supposed to come around and tell us what's going to happen next.

I'm particularly intrigued because I'm not sure what exactly I'm doing here. There's no way that I'm going to participate in another auction.

And if Aiden is going to spend the night with another girl, we're pretty much through.

I know we haven't talked about it and maybe that's a bit unfair, but that's just not where I think our relationship or whatever it is that we have here should be.

Caroline, on the other hand, can't wait for the auction.

"So, tell me about it again," she says excitedly.

I go over what happened last time, and her eyes light up at the thought.

"I still can't believe that I didn't go through with it last time. Man, I was such a coward," she says, shaking her head.

"No, you weren't. This is a crazy thing to do."

"I know, but you did it."

I don't like the way she says *you*, but I let it slide.

"So, you're definitely not doing it this time?" Caroline asks.

"No." I shake my head. "I'm here to see Aiden. And if he doesn't want to see me...I don't know. But I'm definitely not spending the night with another guy."

"You're so sweet," Caroline says. I roll my eyes.

"I mean, I realize that I may be taking this relationship way more seriously than he is, but I haven't had the chance to talk to him about it."

"So, what are you going to do? Just stay in the room?"

"Yeah, I guess so." I nod.

There's a knock at the door. It's Lizbeth.

"Will you two please join me in the main cabin in five minutes?" she asks.

Again, she's wearing a different dress than the one she'd greeted us in.

"Can you tell Aiden that I'm not going to be doing the auction again?" I whisper to her.

She stares at me without saying a word for a moment.

"Please join us in the main cabin," she finally says.

I look over at Caroline.

What the hell is going on?

Will she or won't she give him the message?

I look down at my phone.

Agh, if only I had reception here.

But I don't.

And that means I have no way of talking to Aiden unless Lizbeth or one of the other staff members helps me.

Caroline grabs my hand and ushers me to the main cabin.

Fine, I'm only going because I need to talk to Aiden. But there's no way I'm doing the auction.

Once we walk through the double doors, I see a

familiar sight.

There are women everywhere - on couches, at tables, and all along the bar.

I've seen some of these women at the cocktail party, but many are also new.

All are dressed in high heels and gorgeous dresses.

Glancing around the room, I'm the only one wearing jeans and boots, and I feel severely underdressed.

Lizbeth clinks her glass to get everyone's attention.

The room quickly grows silent.

"Ladies. Thank you all for joining us today. It has really been a pleasure to serve you all."

That word, serve, doesn't throw me as much as it did the first time. Lizbeth's job is to set the mood for the auction and for the general feel of the party. And she is excelling in this position.

Just like last time, she dispels the rumors about the masquerade ball and introduces the auction.

I look around the room, taking in girls' faces as Lizbeth tells them that they are the ones going up on the auction block.

"Mr. Black's auction is nothing like any other auction you might have ever been to, or may have heard of. What makes it particularly special is that, if you choose to participate, you will be the item that's auctioned off."

Lizbeth goes on to explain the basics of the auction, but my mind focuses on one thing.

This isn't just some auction.

It's Mr. Black's auction.

Wait, did I hear that correctly?

And what exactly does that mean?

Is it Mr. Black's auction because he is the owner of the yacht and the host of the party?

Or is it his auction because he plans on participating in the auction just like he did last time?

I mean, that's his right of course. But that's not something that I'm down for at all.

The topic of price comes up again, and again Lizbeth mentions that it's not unusual for women to go for $80,000 to $90,000.

"But you got way more," Caroline whispers. I nod.

"I hope I do, too!"

I flash a fake smile. I don't really care how much Caroline will go for.

All I care about now is whether Aiden will be spending the night with someone else.

After further going into the job of the auctioneer and how the auction will actually take place, Lizbeth hands out the contracts and pens.

"If you are committed to participating, please sign these contracts and hand them back to me," she says.

When she comes around to our table, I pull her aside.

"Can I please talk to Aiden? It's very important," I say.

"Mr. Black told me to tell you that he would like you to participate in the auction," Lizbeth says. "If that helps you make up your mind."

I stare at her, dumbfounded. What the hell is she talking about?

"I don't understand," I mumble, shaking my head.

"No, I can't."

She picks up Caroline's signed contract and smiles at her approvingly. Then she turns her attention to me.

"I would like you to please reconsider," Lizbeth says. "Mr. Black urged me to convince you to participate in the auction."

"C'mon, what are you waiting for?" Caroline nudges me. "Sign the damn thing."

"But what if someone else bids on me?"

I look up at Lizbeth and search her face for the answer. But nothing comes.

"Of course, he's going to bid on you," Caroline says. "He wants you to participate, doesn't he? Just sign it."

"Is that true?" I ask Lizbeth. "He said that he would bid on me if I participate?"

"I really can't divulge that information," she says after a moment.

My mind goes back and forth a million times about the decision.

On one hand, it seems likely that he will bid on me and we will spend another amazing night together.

On the other hand, what if he doesn't?

What if this is just his way of getting rid of me?

No, that can't be right.

I know Aiden.

He wouldn't do that.

So, why wouldn't he just tell me if he will bid on me then?

And why would he want to waste all his money bidding on me in the first place?

I mean, at this point, I'm a sure thing.

We have something more than a one-night stand.

At least, I thought so.

Lizbeth comes around the room with a big stack of signed contracts in her hand.

"Well, what will it be, Ellie?" she asks. I stare at her. I still haven't made up my mind.

"You have to sign it!" Caroline hisses in my ear. "He wants you in the auction. And you want him. So, just do it already."

CHAPTER 3 - ELLIE

WHEN I SUDDENLY REGRET MY DECISION...

*B*ack in my room, I suddenly regret the fact that I was bullied into signing the contract. I should've demanded to see Aiden. Or at least, told Lizbeth that I would go home if I didn't.

But, of course, I didn't want to do that because I want to see him. And I also want to know why he wants to bid on me again.

I mean, is the money really burning such a hole in his pocket that he would bid on me again even though he doesn't have to?

"Oh my God." Caroline bursts into my room. "I'm so excited. How long do you think we have to wait here?"

"I don't know." I shrug. "They have to set up everything and that took some time before."

"Eeek!" She reapplies her lipstick for what seems like the millionth time tonight.

"How are you not more excited about this?"

I stare at her, dumbfounded.

Is she really asking me this question?

"I just don't understand what Aiden wants me to do," I ask. "I mean, does he really want me to participate in the auction? For what purpose? I mean, why does he want to spend money on me? I thought that we were beyond that."

"You're insane, girl." Caroline rolls her eyes.

"No, I'm not. I mean, I thought that we were further along in our relationship now. I don't really want him to pay for my company. I'm not a hooker."

"I see your point. But what if it's just a game to him? I mean, what if he wants all of these guys to bid on you and then he outbids them."

"But what if it's not? What if someone else bids on

me and wins? I'm not sleeping with anyone else tonight."

"Really?"

"Yes!" I say adamantly. "I don't think he would want me to either. But I definitely don't want to. The only reason I came here was because he asked me. But I never thought that I would participate in another auction."

Caroline shrugs.

She doesn't know what else to say.

And I don't know either.

My mind keeps going in loops without really helping me decide on any one thing.

A knock on the door breaks my concentration.

"Hello, girls," Lizbeth says in a sultry voice. "Tonight's auction will be a little different. We would like you to change into this and then meet us in the main room."

She hands us each a box and leaves before we get the chance to open it.

"Wait, Lizbeth." I run after her. "The thing is that I'm

not going to participate in this. I mean, I'm here to see Aiden. He invited me."

"Yes, he invited you. He wants you to participate in the auction."

"What?"

"That's all I know. He asked that you are there on stage tonight."

"And if I decline?"

"Then we arrange for a helicopter to take you home," Lizbeth says slowly. "But just know that Mr. Black will be greatly disappointed."

I want to ask her more questions.

Why is she being so cryptic?

What is all this mystery about?

I mean, why the hell does he want me to do the auction again?

But she turns on her heels and walks away. I follow, but she raises her hand in the air and waves me off.

When I get back to the room, Caroline has already

opened the boxes and scattered the contents on the bed.

Black lingerie - lace panties and bra. Four-inch black heels. The two pieces are identical except for the size of the heels.

"Is this what you wore last time?" Caroline asks.

I shake my head no. "I wore my normal clothes last time," I say.

It takes her a moment to decide before she starts to strip off her dress and change into the lingerie.

I stare at her.

"Aren't you going to change?"

"No." I shake my head.

"Oh, c'mon, you have to."

I hold the bra and panties up to the light. They are definitely made from quality, expensive material.

The problem is that this is lingerie. Something about this whole thing seems off.

Does Aiden really want me to participate in this?

And what if I don't want to.

No, I have to talk to him.

"Don't I look hot?" Caroline asks, twirling her perfect body in front of me.

She's at least three inches taller than I am, and that's being conservative.

So, the way her body fills out this outfit is accentuating in every way.

"Yes, you do."

"C'mon, just put it on. Don't think about it so much, okay? I want to see you in this."

I take a deep breath.

There's no way that this is going to look good at all. I'm pretty certain of that as I change.

But when I look into the mirror, I'm pleasantly surprised that I actually look amazing.

The panties aren't too tight, and the bra is a perfect fit. It elevates my breasts and pushes them up and together unlike any other bra I've owned.

And the heels.

Well, let's just say that they are the most comfortable heels I've ever worn and that's the biggest compliment I can give them.

"Okay, let's go." Caroline grabs my hand.

"No, I'm not going."

"You look amazing, Ellie. Like jaw-dropping amazing. Aiden wants to see you like this. He wants to bid on you. That's why he invited you here in the first place. He wants other men to want you and then he wants to take you home. Don't you see that?"

That is definitely a possibility, of course.

"And what if he doesn't?"

"Don't even think like that," Caroline says, pushing me out of the door. "But if, for some reason he doesn't, then I'm sure you can just back out. I mean these people aren't monsters. This is just a game, right?"

CHAPTER 4 - ELLIE

*J*ust like last time, Lizbeth meets us in the hallway right before we enter and shuttles us out to another room.

This is the waiting area with refreshments in the far corner.

I pour myself a glass of water to quench my thirst. There are fifteen girls in the room - more than there were last time. Every single one is dressed in a bra and panties and black heels.

We're all wearing black. I'm one of the shortest, and the only one without a blowout. Everyone is sitting around chatting.

There's a definite aura of excitement about the whole thing.

"Have you ever done this before?" Caroline turns to the girls at the nearby table.

They all shake their heads no. I look over the girls' faces more carefully and, suddenly, it hits me.

They're all new.

Not a single one is a repeat from last time.

Except me.

"Has anyone else done this before?" Caroline asks a bit louder.

All the girls in the room shake their heads.

"Oh my God, you're the only repeat, Ellie," she whispers to me. "You must've made an impression."

The stage is right in front of us. Lizbeth stands behind the podium in the front of the spotlight.

Just like last time, she's the auctioneer.

Just like last time, I peek out into the room to get a glimpse of the men.

But much to my surprise, there's no one there.

"There were men there last time," I say to Caroline. "They were filling all the seats."

She comes up and looks for herself. Then she points to the mirror dividing the room.

"They must be behind that mirrored partition. It must be some sort of two-way mirror."

I nod in agreement. The mirrored partition gives me some pause.

Why is everything so different from last time?

I was really expecting this to be the same and now I find myself all thrown off.

Lizbeth introduces herself and goes over the rules. She addresses the audience as if they are right there, so they must be.

She tells them that they have to be quiet and press the button when they want to make a bid. She motions to her ear, implying that she can hear them through a hearing device. Lizbeth then says that she will call out the price three times and if no one goes any higher, the girl will go to the highest bidder.

They are then expected to make out a check, money order, or wire transfer to the account of the girl's choice before they're allowed to take her to their cabin.

I pray silently that I'm not called first.

As much as I want to get this over with, I just can't bear to go first. A few minutes later, it starts. Lizbeth calls out the first name. Caroline. My eyes grow wide and I turn to face my friend.

What are the chances?

I expect to see a terrified look on her face, but instead that familiar excited twinkle is in her eyes. She practically leaps out of her seat and prances to the stage in her four-inch heels.

She inhales deeply before stepping onstage. The spotlight focuses on her and she basks in it.

All eyes are on her, just like they are meant to be forever. Lizbeth introduces her by name and states her height. She then starts the bidding at ten thousand dollars.

Unlike last time, I can't see the paddles. There's no one else in the room, but Lizbeth announces the bids as they come in.

Caroline smiles when the bidding reaches fifty thousand, but tries to contain her excitement.

By the time the bidding reaches one hundred thousand, she can't contain her smile much longer. But the bids continue to climb even higher.

There's a slight pause at one hundred and twenty and Lizbeth says that price twice before someone else bids one hundred and thirty.

It stays there for three counts.

"Sold for one hundred and thirty thousand," Lizbeth announces.

Caroline gives a little curtsy as a thank you and leaves the stage.

"Oh my God, Ellie! One hundred and thirty thousand! What kind of money is that? For one night?"

I give her a warm hug of congratulations.

"I mean, it's nowhere close to what Mr. Black paid, of course," she says. "But still."

"That was a fluke," I say, shrugging it off. "It's

awesome to get thirty grand over one hundred thousand. I mean, it is one night."

I try to make her feel better, but I know exactly how competitive Caroline is when it comes to looks, money, and men.

And I also know that the fact that Aiden paid more for me will gnaw at her.

"So, what do you think he looks like?" Caroline asks.

"I have no idea," I say. "Last time, we could see their faces. Plus, we didn't all have to wear the same thing. I guess they're changing things up."

Caroline's eyes sparkle at the prospect. "That's exciting!"

The auction starts again.

One girl goes for ninety thousand and another goes for one hundred and fifty. Caroline stares daggers at her, probably wondering what she has on her.

"Listen, you never know when a particular guy has a particular type. Or maybe he just wants to spend more money than the others to show them up. It doesn't mean that she's better, or hotter, or anything like that."

A familiar meek little man with glasses and a briefcase comes over to our table.

"How would you like your money, ma'am?" he asks, sitting down next to us. Caroline stares at him.

"You can get it as a check, money order, or cash," he clarifies. "Or we can wire it to a numbered account of your choice."

"I have an account in the Cayman Islands," Caroline says. Wow, I did not know that.

"My grandmother set it up when I was little. She was a big tax evader," she explains. "It doesn't have much in it, but I guess that's a good place to put the money if I don't want to pay taxes on it."

I haven't even considered any of the tax implications of all this. Hmm, perhaps it is something to think about it.

I just had the money deposited right into my bank account, but maybe that wasn't the best thing.

So, what should I do now?

I can't very well walk out of here with a money order for all that cash, let alone cash itself.

What if I lose it?

Or get mugged?

I mean, New York City is a much safer city now than it used to be, but it would just be my luck to get mugged the one day I was carrying around one hundred grand in my purse.

"Ellie?" Caroline breaks my concentration.

"What?"

"She called your name."

CHAPTER 5 - ELLIE

WHEN IT'S MY TURN...

My heart immediately jumps into my chest. Oh my God. No, this isn't happening.

"C'mon, get out there." She pushes me out of my chair. Before I get a chance to even gather my thoughts, I find myself on stage with a big spotlight in my face.

When Lizbeth introduces me, I stare straight ahead and silently threaten Aiden.

You better bid on me, I say to myself.

You're the only reason I'm fucking here.

If you don't bid on me...I don't know what I'm going to do.

Slightly out of earshot, I hear Lizbeth say something into her Bluetooth, covering her microphone with her hand.

"Are you sure we can start? But what about..."

I can't quite make out what she says at the end, but something is off. She is clearly reluctant to begin.

"Is everything okay?" I mouth to her.

She gathers her thoughts and nods in my direction.

The bidding begins at ten thousand.

The numbers slowly climb to seventy, ninety, one hundred.

But they suddenly stop at one hundred and ten.

Lizbeth counts to three and then says, "Sold for one hundred and ten thousand."

I nod and walk off the stage.

"Wow, that was a lot less than last time," Caroline jokes.

"I guess Aiden knows that I'm a sure thing," I say.

On the surface, I'm exuding confidence.

It's Aiden.

Of course, it's Aiden who bid on me.

Who else could it be?

But beneath the surface, I'm not so sure.

My hands feel clammy as I sign the paperwork and give them my bank account number.

Somewhere in the back of my mind, I have an uneasy feeling about this.

Why didn't Lizbeth want to start the auction?

Why did she have that hesitation in her voice?

I got a good price, but it wasn't that high.

Does that mean that Aiden just didn't want to pay too much or maybe it wasn't Aiden at all who bid on me?

As soon as the money transfer is complete, another woman comes up to me. She is the same one who escorted me last time.

"I will show you both to your rooms," she says. "Please follow me."

Caroline looks her up and down, winking at the way her breasts are spilling over the top of her corset.

"Where are we going?" Caroline asks, but the woman doesn't reply. She doesn't strike me as the type for idle chitchat.

As I follow behind the woman and Caroline, I get that familiar numb feeling all over my body.

Even though I should be feeling better about everything, I'm not.

Last time, I had no idea what I was in store for. But this time, things aren't exactly crystal clear either.

The woman shows us to the other end of the yacht.

As we make our way there, the rooms get more and more ostentatious and opulent. Again, we pass that large library, filled floor to ceiling with leather-bound books. I wouldn't even be surprised if they were first editions. Again, I have an insatiable urge to run in there and hide.

This is my second time here, and yet I haven't visited the library once. Something about that is very off. Libraries and bookstores are my happy places.

They were always the places I went growing up

when I needed to get away from the world. Whenever anything got too hard to handle and I just needed a break, I always found myself in a little cloistered nook surrounded on all sides by books and stories.

The woman shows Caroline to one of the last doors on the right and me to the door right across from her.

This isn't the same room I had before.

I know because it's a single door instead of a gorgeous French double door.

But once she shows me inside, I see that this room is just as opulent and large as our old suite.

Again, there's a large king-size bed on the far end, a separate sitting area, and large windows looking out onto the blackness of the ocean.

"Your buyer will be here shortly," the woman says. "But first, I have to get you ready."

I try to recollect if that's exactly what I heard before. It is, but it's not.

No, last time, she used his name.

She said, Mr. Black will be here shortly, not
your buyer.

But that doesn't necessarily mean anything, does it?

I have no idea.

I don't know if I'm just trying to read into it
something that's not there or if I'm actually on to
something.

"Do I have to change?" I ask.

She looks me up and down and shakes her head.
"No, you're dressed just as he wants you," she says.
"But he does want you to wear this."

She pulls a night mask from her pocket and dangles
it in front of me. I stare at her. Then she goes over to
the desk and pulls out a pair of black furry
handcuffs.

"Please stand next to the bed post and put your
hands behind it."

I hesitate for a moment, but then do as she says. The
bed post feels cold against my bare back, but the
handcuffs are pretty comfortable.

Once she secures my hands behind the back of the

post, she raises her hands to put the mask over my eyes.

"Is this really necessary?" I ask.

"This is what he wants," she says.

Just like last time, with the mask on my face, I become keenly aware of all sound.

I listen to the woman's heavy footsteps as she exits the room and the way that the yacht creaks slightly with each wave. Somewhere around the room, there is a quiet, disturbing noise that the furniture makes as it settles into the room.

Again, I'm perturbed by the cacophony of sounds that surround me - the same ones that I was completely oblivious to only a few moments ago.

As I lose myself in the moment, my racing mind finally settles down. I had to wear a mask last time as well. I was also tied up last time.

The person who bid on me is Aiden.

I shouldn't have been making myself crazy with all that second-guessing.

Of course, it's Aiden.

Who else would it be?

A loud knock on the door breaks my concentration.

"Aiden?" I ask.

But the person doesn't reply.

The door closes and loud, heavy footsteps approach me.

This must be a game, I decide.

He isn't Aiden now.

"Mr. Black?" I try again.

But the person doesn't reply.

He slowly walks around me.

His footsteps are heavy and deliberate.

My heartbeat goes through the room, the longer he takes to speak.

I feel his eyes all over me, and I'm keenly aware of how my breasts are moving up and down with each rushed breath.

"You're so beautiful," he finally whispers.

I let out a little sigh.

His voice sounds familiar. Not exactly like Aiden's but not completely foreign either.

A moment later, I feel his touch.

He runs his fingertips over my collarbone and the top of my breasts.

Then he runs them up my neck, sending shivers down my body.

"Does that feel good?" he whispers. "Mmm-mmm," I moan, nodding and losing myself in the moment.

"I want to see your eyes."

Slowly, he tugs at my mask and pulls it off my face. Even though the lights in the room are dim, the light still blinds me and it takes me a moment to focus.

When I finally look at the man before me, my body falls into a cold sweat.

"Blake?"

He nods.

"But...what are you...doing here?" I don't know

exactly what I'm saying because my mind is running in circles.

What the hell is Blake Garrison doing here?

"I bid on you," he says proudly, running his finger over my lips. I move my head away abruptly.

"But why?"

"Because I want you. I've wanted you since I saw you at the last auction. But unfortunately, Aiden outbid me that time."

"Where is Aiden?"

"I don't know." He shrugs. "Is it really important?"

Yes, of course, I want to shout on the top of my lungs.

But I'm still stunned by the whole thing.

Why isn't Aiden here?

He has to be here.

He's the one who invited me.

Unless, he wanted me to....spend the night with someone else.

No, the thought of that is unbearable.

"I need to talk to Aiden."

Blake takes a step forward.

He is so close to me I can feel his breath on my lips. He looks deeply into my eyes and licks his lips.

He is definitely attractive, but there's also something menacing and unsettling in his eyes.

There's danger in them, and not the good kind.

Blake brushes his fingers through his dark hair and lowers his chin.

Then he lifts mine up to meet his.

But just as he is about to press his lips onto mine, I pull away at the last moment.

"What are you doing?" I demand.

"I'm going to kiss you," he says with a smile.

"No." I shake my head.

"Ellie, I bid on you. You signed the contract to do anything I wanted tonight."

I shake my head.

I feel tears piling up in the bottom of my eyes.

But I take a deep breath and keep them at bay.

"No, Aiden invited me. I was sure that he would bid on me. I didn't want to participate otherwise."

"Are you two dating?" Blake asks, crossing his hands across his chest.

"No," I say slowly. "Not exactly."

"So, why does it matter?"

"Because I don't want to."

Blake walks around me and looks me up and down.

He's just playing with me.

Toying with me. Right?

"Well, I don't know if that matters," he says after a moment.

My heart sinks.

What did he just say?

I run the words over in my head.

"What do you mean, it doesn't matter?" I demand to know. "This is a voluntary situation."

"Well, actually it's not. You signed a contract. You can't back out now."

My hands turn to ice and my breathing becomes shallow. I don't know what to do.

Should I scream?

Should I yell?

Perhaps, but all I can manage to do is freeze. Somehow, even lifting a finger seems like too great of an effort.

Blake probably takes my lack of emotional outburst as a sign to go ahead.

"I can't wait to do bad things to you," he whispers, running his fingers down my stomach and along my panty line.

When he brushes against my hipbones, something sparks within me. I lift up my leg and knee him in the groin.

"I said no!" I yell, kicking him away from me.

"You bitch!" he yells, toppling over in pain.

A pang of fear rushes through me.

What if I just made things worse?

What if I made him angry?

Well, of course, I made him angry.

But I couldn't very well let him do anything to me without fighting back.

After a few moments of wriggling around in pain, Blake stands up.

His piercing eyes are a shade darker now.

There is so much anger in them that I wouldn't be surprised if steam came out of his ears like from one of those Looney Tunes cartoons.

"You better uncuff me now," I say in the sternest voice possible. "I'm not playing. You can have all of your money back. I'm not consenting to doing anything with you."

I use that word consent on purpose.

In case, there are any cameras anywhere. In this moment, I pray that there are.

"I don't care," Blake whispers, grabbing me by my shoulders. "You already consented."

I try to kick him again, but his legs are too close to mine. He's pressing me against the bed post so hard that my back aches in pain.

"Help!" I scream at the top of my lungs.

He puts his hand over my mouth and I bite down hard.

Luckily, I'm able to bite into the fleshy part and draw blood.

The metallic taste makes me gag, but I'm glad I was able to break the skin.

"Fuck!" He looks at his wounded hand and then smacks me across the face.

Hard.

The impact would've sent me clear across the room, but I'm handcuffed to the bed post and instead it feels like it nearly pulls my arms out of their sockets.

"We can do this the easy way, or we can do this the hard way. Your choice," Blake says, pacing in front of me.

"I mean, I'm not Aiden. But who cares? You didn't know who he was the last time you got auctioned off, so what's the big deal this time? I'm really a nice guy," he says. "Can't you see that?"

My vision is blurry and my head is pounding from the impact.

I manage to nod slightly in his direction.

"Now, c'mon." He comes over closer to me. I feel his breath on my lips and I want to throw up. "Be nice. C'mon, let's have a good time."

I run through all the possible scenarios in my head.

I can kick him again and probably get hit again.

Or I can go along with it.

Just lie there and be quiet.

My whole body trembles in fear. No, this isn't a decision I can make with my head.

Especially now that it's pounding.

This is a gut decision.

Blake takes my non-answer as an answer. He puts his hands on my body again and then presses his lips on my neck.

The nausea in the pit of my stomach comes up my esophagus and I feel like I'm about to vomit.

But before I know it, I lift up my foot and step down hard on his foot with my heel.

Just as he winces in pain, I knee him again in the groin and kick him away from me.

Suddenly, the door to the room bursts open and I see Aiden at the far end.

A moment later, he's on top of Blake, punching him in the face.

"What the hell are you doing?" he demands. "I made it clear that there would be no bidding on her."

But Blake doesn't take the beating lying down.

He is taller than Aiden and heavier.

He uses his weight to his advantage as he punches Aiden back. But Aiden isn't having any of it.

He moves with lightning speed and pins Blake under him once again.

This time, he puts Blake's arms under his knees and punches him in the face over and over until two large security guards run in and pull him off of him.

The rest is somewhat of a blur. Someone uncuffs me and hands me a robe. Someone else puts ice on my split lip and takes a look at the redness around my wrists.

My wrists definitely hurt a lot when Blake slapped me and I got pushed away from the bed post, but I didn't realize just how bad they looked.

Red and bruised, nearly bleeding.

The medic asks me to move my fingers and rotate my wrists. I do as I'm told even though it's quite painful.

The medic also applies some ice to Blake's injuries as he sits across the room with his hands handcuffed behind him.

This time, the handcuffs aren't the playing kind. They are metal. The kind that cops carry around.

When the medic is finished looking Blake over, security guards escort him out of the room. "You're going to pay for this, Aiden!" he yells.

"No, you're the one who's going to pay for this," Aiden yells back. "I told you to fucking stay away from her. You knew the rules. And then I come here and find you..."

His voice cracks and drops off as if the thought of what Blake was about to do to me is too much to bear.

"You care about your company?" Blake yells from outside the room, in the hallway. "About Owl? Well, you better forget about it now!"

"Fuck you!"

CHAPTER 6 - ELLIE

*A*fter everyone leaves, I find myself alone with Aiden. He puts his arms around me and kisses my forehead.

He apologizes over and over, but I still feel numb about what just happened.

"He was about to rape me, Aiden," I say after a moment, looking into space somewhere in front of me. "What the hell happened?"

"I had some work to take care of. And no one was supposed to bid on you, I swear."

"So you did want me to participate in the auction?" I ask.

He nods, looking away. I don't understand. "But why would you want to bid again? I mean, I thought that we were beyond that?"

I don't really know what I'm saying except that I want to say that I thought we were further along than this.

I don't want money to be involved in our relationship anymore.

I want this to be more than it is. But I have no idea if that's what he wants.

"The thing is that Blake is one of Owl's biggest investors. Mainly because he got involved in it so long ago. Back when I didn't have any money."

"Is he your friend?"

"He was. And he wanted you the second that he saw you at the last auction. But I outbid him. I think he was just getting back at me."

I shake my head and walk away. There are words coming out of his mouth, but they still don't completely make sense.

"Ellie, you have to believe me. I'm telling you the

truth. I wanted you to participate in the auction because I thought it would be hot."

"But why did you want me in the auction at all? I mean, I could've just come here and been with you?" I whisper.

Aiden looks away. I see a faint flash of red fill his cheeks. Is this a sign of his embarrassment?

"I wanted to outbid Blake again," he says after a moment. "It's a stupid guy thing. We just got into a disagreement about the direction that Owl will be taking in the future and I wanted to show him up. I wanted to show him that I have the girl. But then I got a very important business call and I couldn't hang up. Owl is free to use as you know, for users. So growing our revenue has become somewhat of an issue. I don't want to bore you with the details."

"No, I want to know," I insist.

"Well, I'm trying to get a bunch of investors on board to try to take it into another direction. I want to monetize the company by selling advertising. And not just to big companies, but to everyday users. Small businesses. People who want to advertise their

Etsy shops, sell their Amazon books, things
like that."

I nod.

"We were having a conference call right before the
auction. And things got a bit heated. That's why I
couldn't call in. I didn't want to put a strain on what
is already a very tenuous and precarious situation,"
Aiden says.

He takes a step forward and lifts my chin up to his.

"But the last thing I thought would happen was that
Lizbeth would go ahead with auctioning you off, and
I never thought that Blake would go that far. I mean,
I knew he was a sexist pig, but forcing you to do
something against your will? I would never
knowingly be friends with someone like that."

There's a desperation in his voice that is quite
convincing. When I look into his eyes, the all-
powerful, alpha guy I knew has all but vanished.

Before me stands a hurt little boy who wants to
desperately convince me of the truth. My head keeps
trying to push him away, but my heart knows that
he's telling the truth.

I break away from his grasp and pace around
the room.

I don't know what to do.

I don't want to forgive him, but I feel like I have to.

"Ellie, I know that what just happened is
unforgivable. I mean, you must've been so scared
and I put you in that situation. But I have to ask you
to forgive me."

He doesn't approach me this time.

Instead, he gives me space. I nod, hearing what he
has to say but not really internalizing it.

The anger that I felt toward Blake is now spilling
over onto Aiden.

I know he's telling the truth, but I don't care.

"Ellie?" he asks after a moment.

"I don't know what you want from me," I finally say.
"I mean, I understand what you're saying, but I'm
still angry. I was tied up here, completely powerless,
in front of that asshole. I mean, I know that this was
an accident, but I'm still fucking pissed."

"I know," Aiden whispers, hanging his head.

"I can't stay here," I say after a moment. "I want to go home."

"Okay," Aiden agrees. "The helicopter pilot went home, but I can call him in. It's no problem."

Fuck, I mutter to myself.

"Do you want me to leave?" I ask.

"No, of course not!" Aiden says quickly. "I want you to stay. But I totally understand why you feel like you have to. Do you want me to call him?"

I think about it for a moment.

A part of me wants to leave. But a slightly bigger part wants to stay.

And not just because the helicopter pilot went home already.

But because of something else.

Something that I feel for Aiden.

"Ellie, what can I do?" Aiden asks, probably sensing my trepidation. "What can I do to make this up to you?"

I think about this for a moment.

"Show me the library."

He smiles out of the corner of his mouth and leads me to the library. It's even more magnificent than I thought it would be.

The ceiling is very tall, just like the rest of the rooms, but this room has elaborate wooden built-in shelves going all the way from the ceiling to the floor.

As soon as I walk in, I'm hit by the strong aroma of brand new books. By the spines, I can tell that many editions aren't new at all, but they are impeccably taken care of.

"Wow, this place is beautiful," I whisper, spinning on my heels.

There are older editions of the classics like The Iliad, and Shakespeare, and there are newer books as well. I walk over to one of the five wooden ladders with wheels at the bottom.

I've seen these in movies, but have never had the pleasure to actually climb one.

"May I?" I ask. Aiden smiles and nods.

I grab a hold of the ladder. Pushing it slightly ahead of me, I step on the lower step and enjoy the momentum that it gathers even though it is a bit brief.

For a second, I'm transported to one of my favorite movies from childhood, *Beauty and the Beast*. That was my favorite movie because Belle was a reader, like I was.

She was a bit of a tomboy and didn't care about guys or getting married. Instead, she always had her nose stuck in a book.

I climb up the steps of the ladder, about halfway up the wall and run my fingers across the hardbacks to the right of me.

My hand lands on the thick large spine of *Atlas Obscura*. I slide it out and bring it back down with me. When I open the book, I press the book to my nose and inhale the sweet aroma of newly printed pages.

"This book is fascinating," Aiden says. "There are so many strange places in the world."

"I've only been on the website," I say, looking at the photo about the island of dolls in Mexico City.

Apparently, the island is something of a memorial to a little girl who died who loved to play with dolls.

"Well, these are quite creepy," Aiden says, reading over my shoulder.

"I've always been somewhat terrified of old dolls," I admit.

We stand here for a few moments, reading about the swimming pigs of the Bahamas and the island of snakes off the coast of Brazil, which people aren't allowed to visit without special permission from the government because it's entirely populated by snakes and no other mammals, including the most venomous snake in the world.

"This book is fascinating," Aiden whispers. "I've read most of it, but I could read it again and again."

"Have you ever seen any of these places?" I ask.

"I've seen a few. But not many."

"I'd love to visit some of these," I announce. "Actually, I'd love to visit them all."

"Why don't you?" he asks after a moment.

That's a very good question. A couple of weeks ago, I

would've had a good excuse. I didn't have the money. But now, things are a bit different now.

"Maybe I will." I nod.

I walk over to a fainting couch at the far end of the room, the kind I've only seen in movies, and lie down, running my fingers across the books above my head.

"So what's going to happen with Blake now?" I ask. Aiden shrugs.

"I don't really know. He's probably going to pull out of the company. He isn't the type to be humiliated and then stick around."

I like the sound of that. "You think I humiliated him?"

"Of course. I mean, you did basically beat him up," he says with a smile on his face.

I won't lie, I like the sound of that.

And this is coming from a girl who has never been in a fight her whole life.

I've always been somewhat of a pacifist.

Or maybe just a wimp.

"And if he doesn't pull out as an investor, I'm going to try to push him out. Even though that's going to cause quite a mess."

"Really?"

He shrugs. "I don't want his money, but Owl sort of depends on it, if you know what I mean. He is the biggest investor and it's already bleeding money. I'm putting all our money into this new advertising strategy and so far it's not really producing a return. At least, not as fast as I want it to."

I nod as if I understand.

"You see, that's what worked so well for Facebook. At first, it was just a social media space where everything was free. And then they had to monetize it somehow. So they started this great advertising platform, which is relatively easy to use for both small and big businesses. And that's where most of their revenue comes from now. And Google, of course, has been doing that as well. That's my plan with Owl."

"So why isn't it working?"

"The platform has some issues. Our reporting isn't as great as Google's and nowhere near as good as Facebook's. And most of the time, we don't spend enough of the advertiser's money per day."

"What do you mean?"

"Well, let's say that the client puts in that they want to spend ten dollars a day on advertising. They create their ad and the audience targeting and ideally the platform is supposed to spend ten dollars or at least about ten dollars. But ours only spends about two dollars or maybe five dollars. It doesn't deliver the ad to enough people in their parameters per day and that's why the spend is so low."

I don't really understand what he's talking about, or how one would even go about making the platform increase its reach, but I nod sympathetically.

He doesn't seem to notice.

After a moment, Aiden gets up and lights the large marble fireplace on the other side of the room.

The light flickers all around the room, making the library look enchanted.

"This place is so beautiful," I whisper, looking

around. Suddenly, every muscle in my body relaxes and my eyelids grow heavy.

It's as if I'm falling under a spell.

"It's my favorite room here," Aiden says, sitting down next to me.

We sit in silence for a bit, watching the flames flicker and catch on one another in front of us.

"The thing is, Ellie," Aiden whispers, "that none of this Owl business really matters now."

"Why not?"

"I don't know." He shrugs. "Just how I feel now. The only thing that I care about is you."

He is sitting so close to me, I can feel the heat emanate from his body.

When I turn my face toward him, I feel his breath on my lips.

He reaches out and brushes his fingers along my bottom lip. His touch feels rough at first, but it quickly softens.

I wait for him to move closer to me, but he doesn't budge. Instead, he remains in place, waiting for me to make a move. After a few moments, I can't bear it any longer.

I move my face closer to his and press my lips onto his. I close my eyes and lose myself in the moment.

As our kiss intensifies, Aiden cradles my face and buries his fingers in my hair. His lips are effervescent. His tongue feels familiar in my mouth.

With one quick motion, he tilts my head and places his lips on my neck. His kisses are slow and deliberate, and I start to feel myself lose all control.

As our legs touch, his hands slowly make their way down my shoulders and toward the small of my back. He pushes me against the couch and climbs on top of me. I let him. I crave him.

My legs open on their own and we intertwine and become one. We roll around, pressing against each other's bodies and losing our hands in each other's hair and clothes. In a few moments, the clothes start to become a hindrance.

Within moments, we struggle out of our clothes and our bodies find each other and collide once again. Aiden kisses me again.

This time his lips are more forceful and as powerful as the rest of his body. The kiss is so forceful it borders on pain, but the good kind. The kind that sends shivers up my body.

I push back into him and feel him rise above me.

Soon, our bodies start to move as one. I love the feeling of his large, hard cock on my pelvic region, toying with me. Teasing me.

I reach for it with my hand and grab hold. But he pulls away as he starts to kiss my breasts and then goes further down my body. He licks my belly button.

My body rises and falls with each kiss. I open my legs and feel the wetness in between my legs.

He slides in without much effort, finally filling me up. I'm so aroused that I feel myself getting close to an orgasm almost immediately.

"Aiden," I whisper, throwing my head back in pleasure.

"Ellie," he whispers into my ear as he moves in and out of me.

I don't care that it has only been a few minutes. I

want to come and I don't dare stop or slow myself down.

A moment later, my legs cramp up. I curl my toes and a warm sensation fills my whole body.

"Oh, Ellie!" Aiden moans a second later, collapsing on top of me after one final thrust.

CHAPTER 7 - ELLIE

THE FOLLOWING MORNING...

*T*he following morning, I wake up curled up on the couch right next to Aiden.

The fainting couch barely fits one person, but somehow we managed to stay the night here together. It feels amazing to wake up next to him.

I love the way he smells and the softness of his features when his eyes are closed. I find myself nestled right in his armpit, and his face is turned slightly away from mine.

His mouth is open just a bit while he breathes in low, deep breaths. I lick my lips.

They are ridiculously dry and my mouth is completely parched. When I finally make the move to get up, I wince in pain.

Sleeping on his shoulder for probably the whole night gave me a big crick in my neck. It hurts to even get up. I force myself to stand up through the pain and slowly start to move my neck from one side to another to work out the kink.

"Oh, hey there, gorgeous," Aiden says, yawning and stretching. "Are you okay?"

"Yeah, my neck just hurts a lot."

"Here, let me help." He jumps up and puts his large, strong hands around my neck.

I wince a little in anticipation of his pushing too hard on my fragile neck, but I'm pleasantly surprised. His fingers are forceful, but deliberate.

It's like they know exactly where it hurts and avoid those spots while releasing pain from the others.

"You have quite a knot here," he says. "Sit down so I can get a bit more leverage."

I sit back down and Aiden towers over me. He puts all of his strength into the knots at the bottom of my neck to work out the kinks.

After a few minutes of going back and forth between wincing and moaning, he lets me go and I try to move my head around. Much to my surprise, I can move it from side to side.

"Oh, wow," I say, effortlessly bending my head from one side to another. "Seriously? How did you do that?"

Aiden laughs.

"Do you have a secret life as a masseuse?"

"No, not at all," he says with a coy smile on his face. "My mom used to deal with a lot of pain all over her back and neck. Ever since I was little, I was the one responsible for giving her massages. When I got to be about ten, I actually got some books out of the library about the right way of doing them. So, yes, you could say I'm somewhat of a self-trained masseuse."

"Well, you're amazing," I say, throwing my arms around his neck and giving him a kiss on the lips.

Unfortunately, our kiss is interrupted by the beeping of his cell phone. Aiden opens the text message and stares at the screen.

For a few moments, he doesn't say anything, but the expression on his face grows grave.

"What's up?" I ask, but he doesn't respond.

I look over his shoulder and read some of the message before he tosses the phone across the room.

"Aiden?"

"That was my lawyer, Blake's pulling out of Owl," he finally says. "And he's taking a bunch of investors with him. Somehow, he managed to convince them that it's a failing company and they are lucky to get out while they still can."

"But it's not, right?"

"No, of course not. We're a bit cash flow low right now, but that doesn't mean anything. We're expanding into new areas and that's why I fucking need that money."

I put my arm around his shoulders.

"But last night you said that it was very likely that Blake would pull out," I say.

"Yes, but I had no idea he would take all of those people with him." He shrugs off my arm and stands up. "Shit."

Aiden pulls on his clothes and paces around the room for a few moments.

"Well, can't you find new ones?" I ask.

"Yes, of course, I can. But it's going to take time. Lots of time. Not that many people have millions of dollars just laying around waiting to be invested into something. As much as that's hard to believe."

I hate the sound of irritation in his voice. He's getting frustrated with me when he has no reason to.

I'm just trying to help.

"I'm sorry," he says after a moment. "I'm just... flabbergasted. I mean, if they all leave, he can trigger a collapse of Owl."

Oh, wow, I shake my head. I had no idea it was that bad.

"Blake has friends in the company and he brought a lot of people on board when no one wanted to listen to me. Besides, Blake is much better with wining and dining potential investors than I am. I don't really have what they call 'people skills.' And if they all pull out...I need that money to keep going with the expansion plans and to make the company solvent. And he knows it. He fucking knows it."

Aiden stops to pick up his phone and dials a number, bringing the phone to his ear.

"Shit, he's not there." He hangs up and sends a text message.

"Who?"

"My lawyer."

"I mean, I pay him good money to fucking answer my calls, but I guess there's something more important right now than the collapse of one of the biggest companies in the world."

A few seconds later, his phone rings again and he talks to his lawyer.

Aiden basically tells him the same thing that he just told me while at the same time covering some of the highlights of what happened last night.

Then, it's the lawyer's turn to talk.

"What did he say?" I ask as soon as he hangs up.

"Nothing really. That he has a lot of phone calls to make. He'll get back to me in an hour. Fuck."

Aiden continues to pace around the room. I try to think of ways to help him.

"So, you have an hour to kill?" I ask. He shrugs, barely acknowledging me.

I get up and walk over to him, stopping his pacing by blocking him with my body.

"Ellie..." He tries to push me away, but I persist. I put my hands on his shoulders and look straight into his eyes.

"You have an hour to kill anyway, right?"

"So?" He shrugs.

"Well, I have an idea of something we can do that's a bit more fun than just walking around the room stressing out about something you can't control."

"What are you talking about?"

I place my hands on his chin and pull it up. His downcast eyes finally meet mine.

"What if you played a little game?" I say slowly. "What would you think of that, Mr. Black?"

I can see it immediately in his eyes that the name Mr. Black means something.

His eyes light up and sparkle for a moment before the rest of his thoughts flood in.

"I don't know," he starts to say, but I put my fingers over his lips and lead him back to his room.

I leave him in the middle of the room and head to the dresser drawer where I remember the restraints came from the last time I was here.

"C'mon," I say, handing him the restraints.

I can see in the expression on his face that a part of him is definitely intrigued by the prospect. But another part is trying to shut it down.

"Listen, let's do this. It will be fun. It will take your mind off things until your lawyer gets back to you. There's nothing else you can do right now, you said so yourself."

He shrugs, reluctantly agreeing with me.

I lead him over to the bed. Facing him, I let the robe fall to the floor. His eyes light up at the sight of me.

He looks over every bit with careful consideration. But unlike my own examination of my body, there isn't one bad thought that pops into his head.

No, it's all admiration and arousal.

"Take off my bra," I instruct.

This isn't exactly how a submissive should act, I guess, but I have no idea what the rules are. All I know is that I want to play, and I want him to play with me.

I stand perfectly still as he walks around and undoes my bra. He pulls it off my shoulders and runs his fingers over my nipples.

They get erect immediately and I feel the warm sensation starting to build in between my legs. Without requiring anymore prompting, he gets down on his knees before me and pulls off my panties.

When I step out of them, his hands run up my thighs. When he pushes them a bit inside of me and then pulls them out and licks his fingers.

"Does it taste good, Mr. Black?" I ask coyly.

He flashes a smile and nods. He walks me over to the bed and puts the restraints around my wrists in the front.

Then he positions me on my back and tells me to lie down. I do as I'm told.

Mr. Black pulls my legs to the edge of the bed and ties a rope around my feet.

I find myself in the lotus position, with my feet touching one another but my knees pointing away from each other, leaving my private area exposed. He takes my arms and ties them to the other side of the bed.

"Is this what you want?" he asks in his deep, confident Mr. Black voice. I nod.

He bends down and puts one of my nipples in between his teeth and bites down a little bit.

"Let me ask you again. Is this what you want?"

"Yes, sir," I say.

"That's a good girl."

I watch as he undresses before me. He flexes his perfect six pack when he takes off his shirt and pulls off his pants.

His tan body glistens under the warm lights of the room. But before I'm done completely admiring his perfect body, he climbs on top of me with one swift motion.

His knees are near my shoulders and his large, erect cock is right next to my lips. He pulls up my head and goes deep inside of me.

I love the feeling of his cock filling up my mouth. It's smooth and rock hard, and as he slides in and out, I feel the outline of him with the tip of my tongue.

I blow him for a bit, but just as I expect him to come inside of my mouth, he pulls out and concentrates his attention on me.

He kneels over the bed and pulls me to one side. Then he puts his fingers deep inside of me and starts to move them in and out.

I'm already super wet from being tied up and from sucking on him and this just pushes me over the edge. I let out a big moan.

I don't really know where it comes from, but somehow a small vibrator appears in his hand.

He presses it against my clit while pushing his fingers deeper and deeper inside of me and massaging me from the inside out.

"Oh, Aiden," I moan when the vibrator hits just the spot and my legs start to cramp up.

"There's no Aiden here." He pulls everything out of me, leaving me clamoring for pleasure.

"I'm sorry. Mr. Black. That feels very good, Mr. Black," I say quickly.

But he watches me and doesn't make a move to re-enter me.

"Would you please keep going, Mr. Black?" I plead. "Please?"

He smiles and nods. A moment later, the vibrator and his fingers are back to sending me to the heights of pleasure.

And just when I think it can't get any better, he pushes one of his fingers inside my butt and continues to move them around.

I feel how tight my pussy and ass wraps around him and the warm sensation starts to build somewhere within my body. I'm getting close.

Just as I'm about to orgasm, he pushes his big hard cock inside of me and starts to thrust in and out.

"Oh my God!" I scream from pleasure. "Oh my God!"

He holds on to my ankles as he pushes in and out of me hard and then we orgasm nearly in unison.

When Mr. Black pulls out of me, my body gets filled with an empty feeling that I'm not familiar with.

I want more of him and I want him back inside. But I just had a mind-blowing orgasm and that should be enough.

"That was wonderful," I whisper, letting out a big sigh.

"Yes, it was." He nods. I expect him to get to work on untying me, but he doesn't.

"But who says that it's over...for you?" Mr. Black asks. I lift up my head to look at him.

"What? Are you serious?"

"I decide when you're done. And just because you came once doesn't mean that this is over."

Shivers run over my body. They are shivers of fear and excitement. Of course, I know that women can have multi orgasms, but I've never had one myself. I've never orgasmed more than once a day before.

"I really don't think I can," I say after a moment.

"You will for me," he says confidently.

He unties my arms and legs and flips me over. He spreads my legs open and positions my butt in the air.

He puts my arms by my sides and ties them to my ankles. My head is turned to one side and squished into the bed.

"How does this feel?" he asks.

"Fine," I mumble into the blankets. "Mr. Black."

Actually, I'm really shocked. Aroused and shocked. This isn't exactly expected, but it's also not entirely uncalled for.

I find myself getting wet again at the prospect of his fingers inside of me.

He slaps my butt a couple of times with his hand. The slaps aren't painful at all, but they are so close to my private area that I feel myself dripping with anticipation.

Then he picks up the vibrator, turns it on, and

presses it against my clit. At first, it feels strange, but quickly my legs start to cramp up.

When he pushes his fingers inside of me, filling me up just like before, I let out a deep sigh of pleasure. Finally, the emptiness feeling is gone.

But that's not all.

One of his fingers makes its way to my ass and inside of my butt. The feeling of being completely plugged by Mr. Black pushes me over the edge. The warm sensation starts to build and I get wetter and wetter.

"Oh, Mr. Black," I moan.

"You have such a tight little pussy," he says, pulling his fingers out briefly and licking me.

He sucks on me and runs his tongue over every fold, sending me to peaks of pleasure. When I feel like I'm about to climax, he thrusts his hand in and out of me, filling me up completely and sending me completely over the edge.

I tense up and scream his name in pleasure at the top of my lungs before my body goes completely limp and I lose all feeling in my legs.

CHAPTER 8 - ELLIE

WHEN I MEET UP WITH CAROLINE

*a*s soon as we're done, Aiden's phone rings again. I can see it in his face that he doesn't want to pick it up, but I urge him to take the call.

It's his lawyer and he needs to take care of his business right now. Especially, since I've been more than taken care of.

When Aiden answers the call, I stretch out on the bed and let my body feel the little sparks that are left over from what had just happened.

There's still electric shocks coursing through my body and getting back to sleep is an impossibility.

"I'm sorry, I have to go to the office," Aiden says.

"Back to New York?"

"Well, yes, but later today. No, I mean my office here. Just down the hall."

I nod, understandably.

"Why don't you get some breakfast?" he suggests, kissing me on top of my head. "We can meet up later."

Breakfast sounds divine, actually. It takes me barely a moment to realize that I'm actually famished.

After going to my room and changing into a pair of jeans and a t-shirt and putting on a fresh pair of panties and socks, I fix the smudged eyeliner under my eyes, run a comb through my hair, and head out of the door.

On my way to the main dining room, I pass another room, which I haven't seen before. It's Aiden's office.

The smell of fine leather, wood, and a mist of citrus spread to the hallway. Aiden's dressed in a pair of wrinkled slacks from last night and a t-shirt. His hair is still a mess and there's a bit of stubble coming in. I doubt that he even had time to brush his teeth.

I peek into the room.

The walls are dark burgundy color, making the

room look much smaller than it really is. The far side of the wall is made of delicate built-in bookshelves, which are a perfect match to the large, imposing desk facing the door. I wave to him, but he's too distracted to notice.

So, I decide to get on my way.

Once I get to the dining room, I see that breakfast is already set up. There's a large buffet selection with four different types of eggs, bagels, fruit, oatmeal, and a variety of bread.

There are two waiters to help you make fresh waffles and pancakes. At the far end, there's a stand for five different types of coffee and tea as well as juice and practically anything else you can think of.

I opt for a plate of creamy scrambled eggs, a piece of toast, and a small bowl of blueberries.

"Ellie!" I hear a familiar voice calling my name from somewhere across the room as I pour myself a cup of English Breakfast tea.

When I turn around with my tray, I see that it's Caroline. She's waving me over to her table.

"Oh my God! I thought I was going to have to have

breakfast all alone," she says when I sit down. "You're the first person who came into this room in close to half an hour."

In case you haven't guessed it, Caroline isn't the type to ever eat at a restaurant alone. She needs people for basic sustenance.

"How was your night?" I ask.

"Fantastic! It was absolutely amazing!" Caroline exclaims.

"Oh my God, I was so nervous, Ellie. I really didn't know if I could do it. But I just told myself, it's going to be fine. The guy will probably be great. Besides, I've slept with a ton of guys who weren't particularly hot and definitely didn't pay me one hundred and thirty thousand dollars."

"That is a lot of money," I agree.

"The thing is that it's not that my family doesn't have money. I mean, I don't have to work for minimum wage at some shitty job. But, still, one hundred and thirty grand doesn't just come to you every day, does it? I mean for one night of sex that you might have had for free anyway."

I nod. She does have a point.

"So, tell me about the guy."

Caroline's eyes light up. "His name is Taylor. He's a bit older. He's in his early forties. But he's really ripped. And hot. He's not very tall, but he's tan and has a really nice body. He definitely doesn't skip the gym."

"That sounds great."

"He's a lawyer. Works for some big Wall Street law firm. His friend invited him to this party. Apparently, he's going through a divorce and his ex-wife isn't really into sex. Not after she had the two kids. So things haven't really been going that well."

"Wow, you really got to know him," I say.

"Yeah, I did. Well, we didn't get down to it right away. This was a new thing for both of us. So, we spent a few hours getting to know each other first."

A few hours.

Wow.

I am actually taken aback by that.

He must've made an impression because I doubted

that Caroline spent a few hours getting to know anyone before.

"He told me all about his ex and the divorce. It was kind of intense actually. I mean, she's taking him to the cleaners over the whole thing. They've been together forever. Like thirteen years."

"So how was...everything else?" I ask.

"You mean the sex?" Caroline asks.

Her eyes light up at the thought.

"It was amazing. We did it twice! Ordered food after the first time and then did it again. I barely slept as you can imagine. But he did make me come twice."

"Wow," I say. "I don't remember a guy who made you orgasm even once recently."

"I know, right?" She shakes her head. "I think guys our age just don't know what they're doing. Or they're too much into themselves. But Taylor...oh my God, Ellie. He really took his time. He was there for me. He's definitely a keeper."

I can't help but smile.

I don't remember the last time Caroline has ever

said that about a guy except for her boyfriend from high school who broke her heart.

But I'm happy for her.

It's about time she got a little less jaded about men. I mean she is only a woman in her early twenties. It's not healthy to hold opinions of a divorce in her forties at her young age.

"So, do you think you'll see him again?" I ask.

She takes a sip of her coffee, nodding.

"We exchanged numbers and he said that he wants to see me again. In the city."

"That's great."

"I mean, I know that all men say that. Oh, hell, I've said that to numerous guys myself without ever having any intention of following through. But I really hope he does. I really like him, Ellie."

———

AFTER BREAKFAST, Caroline and I head back to our rooms to get our stuff. Lizbeth has arranged for the helicopter to take us back home.

Once I have all of my stuff, I stop by Aiden's office to say goodbye but he's nowhere to be found. Then I knock on his suite door and check for him in the library.

But he's not there either.

Hmm, that's odd.

But I guess he's busy, I think to myself. I mean, yes, of course, I know that he's busy. His company is going up in flames, partly because of me.

But I still can't help feeling a bit disappointed at the fact that we can't say good-bye and exchange a kiss. My disappointment is confounded by the fact that Taylor comes out to the helicopter pad to see Caroline.

He gives her a warm hug and a long kiss and whispers something in her ear.

Caroline wasn't lying.

He's definitely easy on the eyes, even for a much older guy.

The flight back is uneventful. Caroline continues to gush about Taylor all the way back, and I listen unenthusiastically, lost in my own thoughts about Aiden.

Why didn't he say good-bye?

When will I see him again?

Will everything be okay with this whole mess with Blake?

Finally, when we're about to land in Manhattan, Caroline asks me about my night. It catches me a bit off guard and, for a moment, I debate whether I should mention Blake at all.

But I feel embarrassed about the whole thing. I mean, being tied up and having a blindfold over my eyes and having the wrong guy come in the room.

I know that it's not my fault, but I can't help feeling like I did something wrong. In the end, I decide to pass on it. It should've never happened.

I don't blame Aiden for it anymore. I know it's all Blake's fault. But I still have trouble admitting the truth out loud.

"So, he just showed up to your room? And everything was...fine?" Caroline asks.

I nod. "Yes, it was. It was great actually. Very sexy,"
I lie.

"See, I told you! I knew it. Of course, you had
nothing to worry about. I mean, Aiden wouldn't let
someone else bid on you at his party on his yacht.
What kind of guy would do that?"

My cheeks flush from embarrassment, and I turn
away from her so she doesn't notice. A part of me
wants to stand up for Aiden.

I mean it was an accident. And he was very angry
about it. But another part knows that she's right. It
should've never happened. Especially, if he knew
that Blake had his eye on me.

Suddenly, I consider confessing to the truth.
Caroline and I are good friends, and we don't keep
things from each other. But the more she talks about
how of course I had nothing to worry about, the less
inclined I am to tell her the truth.

CHAPTER 9 - ELLIE

WHEN I SEE MY PARENTS AGAIN...

*L*ater that evening, I get a text message from my mom saying that she can't wait to see me for dinner.

Shit.

I completely forgot that I had made plans a week ago to have dinner with her and my stepdad. I consider trying to get out of it, but then decide that it's going to be more trouble than it's worth.

Besides, I don't have any plans for tonight anyway, and the most I can push her off is a day or two.

I meet Mom and Mitch in their apartment on Fifth Avenue. They are in the city to catch Hamilton on Broadway and then they're going back to Greenwich, Connecticut at the end of the week. I haven't been

here in two weeks, which is kind of a long time
for us.

Usually, I have a weekly dinner with them just to
catch up on what's going on. We established the
routine when I started at Yale and it was nice to just
keep going with it.

Mom opens the door and gives me a warm hug.

"You look great!" she says.

"You, too," I say.

And she does. She's a small woman, about five feet
five, with a short blonde bob like Marilyn Monroe's.
She's tan and her eyes aren't as tired as they
once were.

But that's to be expected, I guess.

Her life with Mitch has been considerably less
stressful than her life with my dad. They got
divorced when I was eight and she met Mitch soon
afterward.

He had lots of money and wasn't shy about spending
it on her. He wined and dined her and after they got
married, she quit her job as a teacher.

Mitch greets me in the dining room with a scotch on the rocks in his hand. He isn't much of a drinker, meaning I've never seen him drunk, but then again, a night doesn't go by without him having a drink either.

He's a few years older than my mom and has a few gray hairs around his temples. He's quite attractive for a man his age, and he enjoys wearing expensive suits and shoes.

When my mom pours us two glasses of red wine and hands me one, Mitch puts his arm around her and gives her a little hug. All of these years later, it is still clear to me that they are as in love as ever.

The thought of that warms my heart. But it also gives me a little pang in the pit of my stomach. Unlike my mom, my dad has not been so lucky in love.

He keeps mainly to himself and even if he does date on occasion, he has never introduced me to anyone in all of these years. I think he never got over my mom and still pines for her. He even keeps pictures of the two of them together on his mantel.

"How's Annabelle?" I ask when we sit down for dinner.

Annabelle is Mitch's daughter from his first marriage. Her mom died when she was very little and my mom basically raised her.

I'm five years older than Annabelle and we used to be very close. But she started to pull away from me when she started high school.

The older that Annabelle got, the more difficult it became to maintain a relationship with her. She got kicked out of a couple of schools and started dressing entirely in black, painting her nails black and her face white.

There aren't supposed to be many goths around anymore, but Annabelle somehow found and embraced the culture. I keep thinking that she will grow out of it, but Mom and Mitch aren't so sure.

"Her college applications are due in a couple of months," Mom says. "I'm helping her fill them out."

By helping her, I know exactly what my mom means. Annabelle isn't interested in college and Mom and Mitch are insisting that she attend. So, Mom has taken it upon herself to fill out the applications.

"Where is she applying?" I ask, helping myself to a big portion of Caesar salad.

Mom makes incredible homemade vegetarian Caesar dressing, which is to die for. It's one of my favorite things to eat when I'm home.

"A lot of smaller liberal arts schools," Mitch says. "I think those should be a good fit for her. We don't want her to get lost in a big school."

I nod. That makes sense.

Annabelle is rebelling, hating everything about our parents.

Maybe going to a big school isn't the best thing for her.

"Princeton?" I ask about Mitch's alma mater. He shakes his head with disappointment.

"I'd have to buy them a building to get her in at this point. And I don't have nearly enough money for that."

"Cornell might still work," Mom says optimistically. "Or maybe Dartmouth. If they see her rebellion as a way of challenging social norms that she has grown up with."

I nod.

"But we also have Oberlin, Middlebury, Bowdoin, and Davidson in North Carolina," Mom says.

"Any safety schools?" I ask.

"She says that if she absolutely has to go to college, she doesn't want to go anywhere warm or too sunny. She seems to like Vermont a lot and Maine, so Mom is filling out applications to the University of Vermont and the University of Maine," Mitch says, taking a sip of his scotch.

"Those sound like good options," I say.

I chuckle to myself, trying to imagine Annabelle at the University of Florida or Miami.

All that fun in the sun has to become contagious at some point, right?

"Have you talked to her recently?" Mom asks.

They both look up at me hopefully. I know that they think if anyone can connect with her at this point it would be me, but I shake my head and look away.

"No, not recently. I called her a few times and texted. But you know Annabelle. If she doesn't want to be reached, then she can't be reached."

"We're just so worried about her. I mean, you don't think she's into doing drugs or anything like that?"

"She probably smokes pot, Mom," I say.

"We know that. Most kids nowadays do anyway. But I don't mean pot. I mean harder drugs. I keep reading all this stuff about the opioid epidemic. The number of people who get hooked on prescription pills and then end up on heroin...it's just frightening. And not just hooked. Many of them die. It's so easy to overdose nowadays."

I nod sympathetically. I don't really know what else I can do. The opioid epidemic is a real problem, but not one that I can really solve.

"That's my only problem with those large state schools in New England," Mitch says. "There are so many people suffering with addictions there."

"Well, c'mon, let's be fair," I say. "It's not like people in New York don't also struggle with addiction. Do you think she'll want to go to some school in New York City?"

Mom and Mitch shrug.

"Basically, she doesn't want to go anywhere," Mom

says. "But we're not willing to support her just lounging around doing nothing all day. She needs to get an education. So, if she wants us to continue to support her, she'll have to go to college. And I'm not sure that New York City is the best place for her. Too many distractions, if you know what I mean."

Of course, I do. Especially, for someone like Annabelle. Annabelle was always a lot more outgoing than I was.

While I was happy to spend my days with my head in a book, Annabelle needed to be out there socializing with other kids. She's a social butterfly.

Actually, she's a lot like Caroline.

But something must've happened when she got to high school to make her shut down so much and start to rely exclusively on a very small group of kids for friends.

"Okay, enough about your sister," Mitch says when it's time for the main course.

The grilled salmon looks delicious.

I help myself to a generous portion and get some

more Caesar salad as well. "Tell us about you. How's your job? What's new?"

Ah, me.

Hmm, where do I even start?

Well, since we last met, I auctioned myself off to the highest bidder, made more money than most people make in five years, and quit my job to focus on writing romance.

Oh, yeah! And I also started dating a billionaire who likes to tie me up.

But I can't very well come out with all of that at once.

I try to think of somewhere to stagger the conversation and reveal just enough of the truth so that I'm not lying without actually telling them anything.

"I haven't seen any of your recent quizzes," Mom says. "I love taking them! Can you forward me some?"

Mom has always been very supportive of my writing. She loves to read any stories that I publish and has been a devoted taker of all the BuzzPost quizzes that I made up.

Shit.

I guess this is as good a time as any to tell them that I'm not working there anymore.

"Actually, I quit that job," I say, taking a sip of my wine.

"What? Why?" they ask almost in unison.

"I didn't like my boss. She's the daughter of the owner of BuzzPost and she was just...too demanding. Plus, writing quizzes wasn't exactly my dream job."

"But that's a great company. They're really up and coming, Ellie. You could've worked your way to better assignments," Mom says.

"Oh, c'mon, writing quizzes? After going to Yale, you really think that's the best she could do?" Mitch asks Mom. "Besides, now she can really think about going to law school."

I take a deep breath.

I don't know what's more annoying. Mom being overly supportive of my writing and being upset that I wasn't at my crappy entry-level job anymore or

Mitch seeing this as an opportunity to shove law school down my throat once again.

"No, I don't want to go law school," I say as clearly as possible. "I definitely want to be a writer. And I'm working on something now."

"You are?" Mom's eyes light up.

"Well, yes. Something longer."

"That's wonderful. I'd love to read it when it's done."

And there lies the problem, I say to myself.

"Actually, it's a book. A novel. But I'm not sure if it's... for everyone," I say.

I want to say it's definitely not for you, but that would sound too rude.

"What do you mean?"

"Well, I've been doing some reading and there are lots of people who are self-publishing nowadays. And their books are doing quite well. Selling really well, I mean."

"So, you're planning on self-publishing your book?" Mom asks. "Don't you want to at least submit it to some agents? Maybe you'll get lucky."

Shit.

This isn't exactly the direction that I wanted the story to go in.

I didn't mean to go into this whole self-publishing direction. That's just something that I have been thinking about on my own, but not something that I needed to share with them at this point.

How the hell did it just slip out?

"It's not really mainstream kind of stuff," I say after a moment. "What I mean is that it's a romance. There is a huge indie romance community online. Lots of readers and they love these self-published authors. So, I want to try my hand at writing something like that."

"Romance?" Mom asks with a sour expression on her face.

I look over at Mitch.

He's not much of a reader for pleasure and I doubt that he even knows who Danielle Steel is. But, Mom, who is a lover of the crime fiction genre, definitely doesn't approve.

"I didn't plan it that way, but then I started writing

and it really became a full-fledged romance. Just thought I would try something new," I say. "Besides who knows? Maybe it will actually sell unlike my other stories."

"Oh, Ellie." Mom shakes her head. "I love your short stories."

"I like them, too," I say. "And I can still write more in the future. But for now, I really want to focus on something that someone else will enjoy. I've been reading a lot in the genre and it's really dynamic. There's so much experimentation. The authors are really trying new things. The style of narration, for example, is miles ahead of what's going on in literary fiction. Plus, the amount of sexual content...is liberating."

I choose my words carefully.

I don't know exactly how to approach the topic, but being straightforward is probably best.

My parents aren't exactly prudes, but I'm also not entirely sure if they are well-versed in just how explicit some of it gets.

"You know me," Mom says. "I've never read Fifty Shades of Grey, but-"

"Yes, I know," I interrupt before she gets the chance to continue her thought. "But those kind of books are really popular. And you wouldn't believe how many regular people, mostly women, are making a really good living writing that kind of fiction. I mean, they don't have publishers and they're doing it all on their own. I still have a lot to learn, but I'm reading lots of books and blogs and even thinking of signing up for a course on book marketing. There's a lot of work involved."

"So, is this why you quit your job at BuzzPost?" Mitch asks, finishing his glass of scotch and pouring himself another.

"Not exactly," I say. "But yes, it's a big part of it. I was sick of writing those quizzes. And they weren't paying me much anyway. The thing is that I think I can really do this. I mean, why not? I can write fast and I can write compelling characters. And maybe someone will want to read them?"

A part of me regrets going into the whole business plan so early in the process.

In reality, there are tons of books on Amazon that no one reads and that's not because they're not any good, but because the authors don't have the right marketing plan. And I have no idea whether my approach to marketing will actually result in sales.

But I also wanted to share with my parents what I'm actually doing instead of harping on the fact that I no longer work at BuzzPost.

Besides, I can't very well go into what happened at the yacht and how much money I now have in my bank account. We will have to go into that a bit slowly.

"Well, I don't think there's any harm in trying," Mitch announces, much to my Mom's dismay. "I mean, what's the worst that can happen? You crash and burn and then actually give law school some thought?"

He says the last bit in a joking manner, but I know that he's not joking. He's dead serious about what I should be doing with my life.

He used to push me to look for a job in banking, saying that he could place me in one of the biggest investment banks around and put me on the track to make a comfortable six figures within a year or so, with bonuses.

But when I rejected that idea, then he came up with law school.

I appreciate his input, of course.

But not his approach.

I mean, I know that he just cares about me. And we have more in common with one another than he does with his real daughter, Annabelle, but that doesn't mean that he knows what's good for me in life. I have to make my own decisions and live by those decisions.

I have no idea how romance writing as a business will work out. All I know is that I love writing, and I love the idea of someone actually reading my work.

I used to write a lot of short stories and submit them to literary magazines, which no one reads in the first place, except for other starving writers. And that's if they even got accepted, which most of the time they didn't.

And the thought of having readers writing me and telling me how much they enjoy my work just seems too good to be true.

"Well, enough about work," Mom says, changing the subject. "What else is going on with you? Caroline?"

I shrug. "Nothing much. Caroline is Caroline. Having a lot of fun as usual."

"You know you could learn a thing or two from her," she says. "I know that she can be a little flaky at times, but her carefree nature makes it easier to live life, you know?"

I nod and hang my head a bit. Mom is a worrier and it's in her nature to worry about her only daughter.

"I'm carefree," I say as convincingly as I can.

"You? Are you serious?" Mom asks with a scoff.

I can't stand the criticism anymore, even if it's veiled in a compliment. "So, on one hand you're worried that I'm not pursuing my calling as a serious writer. But on the other, you think I should be less serious and more carefree? So, which is it?"

I rarely come out and say exactly what I mean to Mom or Mitch for that matter. Mainly because I don't like confrontation and I would much rather just listen to their advice and then do what I think is right.

"Well, I just mean..." Mom starts to say. I wait for her to continue, but I clearly caught her in a trap. "You know what I mean."

I know that you just need to criticize me in some misguided effort to make me more of a person that you think I should be, I want to say.

But I keep this bit to myself.

CHAPTER 10 - AIDEN

WHEN EVERYTHING FALLS APART...

My phone rings again and again. I look down at the screen and see that it's Ellie. She has been calling a lot in the last few days, but I can't bring myself to answer.

I can't bring myself to face her. She did nothing wrong. She was a victim. I should've been there for her before Blake did any of that.

As it turned out, Blake is an even bigger asshole than I ever suspected to him be.

I will never forgive him for what he did to Ellie. But it's not like he's out there begging my forgiveness either.

Blake Garrison is Owl's biggest investor.

He invested in my company back when it was nothing but a computer in my dorm room. It's not like he put a lot of money up back then, but he still got a big stake, mainly because he's the only one who put up any money at all. And now, well, everything is pretty much fucked.

He's mad at me for how I treated him at the yacht and there's no way that I'm ever apologizing.

He was the one who was at fault. So, we're pretty much at a standstill.

He's angry and pissed, probably because he's embarrassed at how he acted. But I know him. He's a very petty person who doesn't let grudges go.

If someone crosses him, or if he thinks that someone crosses him, he'll do anything to take them down, even if that means that he will lose money doing it.

I turn on the TV.

It's more of an act of masochism than anything else. I rarely watch the news, let alone a channel like CNBC which reports on news from the stock market.

But my company is going down in flames and I'm morbidly curious.

An animated bald man with a sour expression on his face reports that Owl has been devalued a billion dollars on the exchange.

The stock price is plummeting and everyone who bought high are selling their shares quickly. By pulling out of Owl, Blake has started an avalanche.

The amount he had invested was a lot, but what he mainly did by pulling out is scare off all the rest of the investors.

We were pretty short on cash anyway, trying to open up new advertising revenues, but this has pushed us over the edge.

My phone rings again. It's Ellie again. Again, I hang up. I just can't deal with her right now. It's not even her. I can't really deal with anyone right now.

I'm losing everything that I've worked so hard for and I have no idea how to stop the bleeding. I go to the liquor cabinet and pour myself a big glass of scotch. No rocks.

I take a few big gulps and let the dark liquid coat the back of my throat. The drink doesn't change anything, of course, but my outlook.

And that's enough for now.

It's more than I can even ask for.

CHAPTER 11 - ELLIE

*H*e's not picking up. I hang up the phone for what feels like the millionth time since I started calling him a few days ago.

The first time I called him was the night I got back from my Mom's. I was upset over her approach to my writing and I needed to tell someone.

I knew that if anyone understood, it would be Aiden. But he didn't answer. At first, I didn't think it would be a big deal. I mean, maybe he was busy.

But then I called him the following afternoon. I left messages both times and both times I didn't get as much as a text. That night I also texted.

The more time that passed, the more anxious I grew. I knew that I was annoying him. I knew that he was getting my calls. But I didn't know why he wasn't answering.

And I couldn't stand it.

Why wasn't he answering?

It has been a few days now and he still won't answer. My worry and anxiety has slowly morphed into disappointment and anger.

And a lot of questions started to creep in. Maybe he isn't as okay with what happened back at the yacht. Yes, we made love - or rather, we had sex. But maybe that was all it was.

Who the hell knows?

Aiden is one person when he's with me and another person when we're apart.

I mean, what do I really know about him?

Maybe the person I spent my time with on the yacht isn't really him at all.

Or maybe it's just a version of him.

I mean, aren't we all just versions of ourselves and it's up to us who we choose to become in a particular circumstance?

With all of these thoughts swirling in my head, I find it incredibly difficult to write.

As opposed to before, when words just spilled out of me, probably powered by the muse which Aiden has inspired, now I can't write a single word.

All of my thoughts concentrate on Aiden and his whereabouts, and I can't distract myself even for a second to think about my characters and their petty problems.

And it's with all of this on my mind that I find myself wandering the streets of New York this afternoon going nowhere in particular. The weather turns cold with the wind slicing in between the tall buildings, funneling through the narrow streets.

I regret not grabbing a hat before I left, but I honestly thought that the days were still going to stay warm for a bit longer.

After walking mindlessly around a bookstore, leafing through a few books, but picking up none of them, I find myself in front of Aiden's building.

I can't believe that I walked all this way lost in my own thoughts, but it's as if my feet carried me here all on their own. Without even my consent.

The doorman remembers me and calls up to Aiden's apartment. I hear Aiden answer and barely make out his muffled words. The only thing I do know for sure is that he isn't entirely excited to see me.

His voice sounds detached and somewhat confused.

The doorman calls the elevator for me and I ride up by myself. I look at my own reflection in the mirrored elevator and ask myself what the hell am I doing here? I mean, this guy isn't taking my calls.

Why the hell am I here confronting him?

He has the right to never call me again.

This is New York.

People don't owe each other much, even if they have had a few nights of glorious sex together.

I knock on his door.

A few moments pass without an answer. Suddenly, it occurs to me that my humiliation might not have any bounds.

What if, after all this, he doesn't answer the door?

I mean, he didn't answer my calls, so this wouldn't be that out of bounds.

Shit.

I stand in the hallway and wait.

How long should I wait?

I probably shouldn't wait long, but I want to see him. My arm lifts up without my explicit consent and knocks on his door again. This time, more forcefully.

Stop it, Ellie, I say to myself.

What the hell are you doing?

Why are you harassing him?

I don't have an answer to that except that I need an explanation. We had such a good time. He really opened up to me.

And I opened up to him.

So, why is this happening after all this time?

He can't tell me that I had just imagined all of that. No. I won't believe it.

When I'm about to turn away, the door swings open. The man who faces me is Aiden. But he's also not the Aiden I saw only a few days ago. His hair is all out of place. He is dressed in an old t-shirt and a pair of ragged shorts. His barefoot feet look out of place on the fabulous, newly polished floor.

Holding a bottle of scotch in one hand, he offers it to me. I turn him down immediately, he shrugs and takes a swig. His eyes look sunken in, and his skin has lost all of its luster. He looks like he hasn't slept in days. All of my anger with him dissipates at the sight of him and is quickly replaced by worry.

"Aiden?" I whisper.

He waves me inside. I follow him down the hallway, very well aware of the fact that he isn't stable on his feet. Aiden can't walk in a straight line and even trips over thin air near the kitchen counter.

"What's wrong?" I ask, louder this time and more forcefully.

"Nothing." He shrugs. "What could be wrong?"

He downs another gulp of the scotch before I pull the bottle away from him.

"Hey, if you're not going to drink that, I don't see why you have to take it," he says slowly. His words are forced. They require too much thought. He's clearly very, very drunk.

"What happened?" I ask. I know that he's very inebriated, but I also want to find out why before he passes out completely. One thing is for sure, he's not drinking anymore tonight.

Aiden makes his way slowly to the living room, wavering from side to side. There are a few moments when I'm sure that he is about to fall and crack his head open, but somehow he catches himself in time and steadies himself.

After plopping down on the couch, he flips on the television.

"Aiden, what's wrong?" I sit down next to him, taking his hand in mine. "I don't want to watch TV right now. We need to talk about this."

Raising his arm slowly and with great effort, he points his index finger at the screen. I turn to look. Suddenly, it all makes sense.

There's a panel of four talking heads and they're all forcefully and with great glee discussing the downfall of Owl. One suggests that there may be a way to recover. But the other ones just keep bringing up the fact that the company lost over a billion dollars within a span of one day and no one has ever recovered from that kind of fall before.

"Oh my God," I whisper. I don't really know what else to say. I rarely put on cable news and I never watch CNBC. I had no idea any of this was going on.

"Aiden?" I turn to him. He slouches down on the couch and closes his eyes. His arm is over his eyes.

"But how is this happening?" I ask. He shrugs, but says nothing.

I can tell that he has already had way too much to drink. Asking him any more questions tonight will be a rather futile exercise. Instead, I pull him up to his feet and walk him to his bedroom. His feet drag on the floor and I feel like I'm going to drop him at any moment. But somehow, with great struggle, we eventually make it there. I pull open the covers, sit him down on the bed, and then lift his legs up to the mattress. At first, he struggles a bit, but quickly gives up. I pull the covers over him and adjust his pillow a bit. His eyes are closed by the time I turn off the light on the nightstand.

I head back to the living room and sit down on the couch. The television is still on and the talking heads continue to argue. I listen for a while, completely at a loss as to what to do. How the hell did this happen? I keep asking myself. The talking heads also wonder about all the things that could've gone wrong, but they keep coming back to one thing. Blake Garrison, Owl's biggest investor, had pulled out. There are rumors that he called other investors who he got in on the deal to pull out with him.

"So, what does Garrison know that we don't know about the inner workings at Owl?" one of the suits on TV asks.

"He knows that something very bad is going on at Owl. Maybe something that SEC even needs to investigate," the other one says.

The SEC? I want to scream at the television. Are you fucking kidding me? You want to know why Garrison pulled out? Because Aiden Black caught him almost raping a helpless woman on his yacht and Blake was embarrassed. It has nothing to do with Owl at all. Of course, I know that no one on TV knows any of this. And beyond that even, I don't know if they should know.

I get up and pace around the room. Perhaps, they

should know. Maybe I need to come out and say something. Maybe I even need to hire a lawyer. Then they wouldn't be blaming Owl. And maybe that can stop some of the bleeding. At least, get some of the investors to stick around. But if I come out with any of this, then I have to tell everyone everything. I would have to go on the record about the auction and the Daily Post would have a field day with me - a nice girl with an Ivy League education putting myself up on a sex auction. Shit. My thoughts swirl around in my head, going back and forth between ideas. One minute, I'm convinced that I need to go on CNBC and set the record straight and another minute, I want to wait it out.

There is one thing that I'm sure about. I can't do anything rash tonight. I have to wait until Aiden sobers up. I need his input. I mean, all of this is about his company, his yacht, and his party. I'm not sure how open he would be to the whole idea of the fact that he auctions off girls to the highest bidder. That isn't exactly fodder for better stock prices.

I take a deep breath and lie down on the couch. It's so big and wide and comfortable that it pulls me into a little cocoon. I turn off the television and put in my earphones. I turn on one of my favorite playlists on Spotify and let it lull me to sleep. Within a few minutes, I curl up in between the big, overstuffed pillows and the world doesn't seem so dark and gloomy anymore. Maybe everything will be okay after all, I decide. And even if it won't, at least I don't have to worry about it much anymore. I can't change anything tonight anyway.

One of my favorite songs comes on. It's a violin cover of "A Thousand Years." I listen to its slow progression and how deliberately it builds with each bit. I don't know anything about music or how it works, I just enjoy it. My eyelids start to feel very heavy and I quickly fall into a deep sleep.

CHAPTER 12 - ELLIE

THE FOLLOWING MORNING...

*W*hen I wake up many hours later, the sun is pouring in through the windows.

For a brief moment, I'm confused as to where I am. This place looks completely foreign and it takes me a minute to realize that I'm at Aiden's.

I climb off the couch, stretch my arms above my head, do one sun salutation, and then walk to the master bedroom.

I knock lightly, but no one answers.

I let myself in and see that Aiden is almost in the exact same position that I left him.

Luckily, there is no vomit next to the bed, but he still looks a mess.

A gorgeous, beautiful mess, but a mess.

His hair is tossed and his face is the palest I've ever seen it. It's so pale, it's bordering on shades of green. I sit down on the bed next to him and push on him a bit.

After a few strong shoves, he opens his eyes and moans.

"Good morning, sunshine," I say jokingly.

He squints in pain from the light that comes in through the window.

"Oh my God, my head," he says very slowly.

"Yeah, you had quite a lot to drink last night."

Aiden shakes his head in disbelief. "I did? I feel like shit."

"I'm going to put a pot of coffee on," I say. "Why don't you try to get up and wash your face?"

I walk out of the room slowly, debating whether I should help him into the bathroom or not. But as soon as I start the coffee going, I hear him somewhere behind me, struggling with walking about.

A few minutes later, he staggers out of the room. I pour him a large and a very strong cup of coffee.

He must've thrown some water on his face, but not wiped it with a towel, as it's still wet.

At least his eyes are a little more open and alert now.

"Ellie, I'm really sorry about everything," he says slowly, taking a sip. "Shit, this is hot!"

"I know, it came straight from the pot," I say, blowing on my cup.

"I'm just really sorry for being such a fucking mess."

"Listen, you have nothing to be sorry for," I say. But then decide to reword my words. "All I wish is that you hadn't shut me out. I mean, I didn't know anything that was going on with you. I thought that you didn't really want to see me anymore."

A big part of me feels very petty for even bringing all of that up.

I mean, here he is with his company blowing up in

front of him, and here I am complaining that he didn't call me back.

But still, I can't help but feel how I feel.

"I should've called," he says. "I'm sorry."

I nod and put my arm around his shoulder.

"It's fine. I know you have been going through a lot. I just wish you'd told me about it. I mean, I couldn't really do anything. But still. Please don't shut me out."

I realize how pathetic I sound, but I can't help it.

"I was just really embarrassed," Aiden says after a few moments of silence. "I really didn't think that Blake would do this. I mean, I didn't think that he would cause this fucking avalanche of shit."

"He's such an asshole," I say.

Aiden nods, flashing me a smile.

Despite how tired and worn out he looks, his teeth remain a pearly white.

For a moment, I lose myself in the curve of his mouth and the gentleness of his eyes.

The graceful strength of his hands makes my own hands grow weak.

He takes another sip of his coffee and then looks up at me again.

The sunshine that streams in through the window gives him a halo above his head even though he's pretty far from being a saint.

"Ellie," Aiden says very softly.

His voice drifts off at the end. I look into his eyes and wait.

"I love you."

The words hang in midair in between us as if suspended on a string.

That was the last thing I'd expected him to say.

Despite the fact that I've been feeling like I may be falling in love with him, too.

"You don't have to say anything," he adds quickly. "It's just how I feel. It's how I've felt for a while now and I thought you should know."

I find the confidence and nonchalantness in his voice disarming.

He is standing completely exposed in front of me, holding his beating heart out in front me, without a worry in the world.

"I think..." I start out slowly. "I think, I love you, too."

He smiles out of the corner of his mouth.

"No, that's not right," I correct myself. "That's not true. I don't think...I know."

I take a deep breath. This isn't coming out exactly right.

"I love you, too," I finally say what I should've said all along.

"You do?"

I nod.

Aiden presses his lips onto mine.

I open my mouth and welcome him inside.

When we pull away from one another, the day doesn't seem so gloomy after all.

At least, not for me.

But when I glance over at Aiden, I can still see that he has the whole world on his shoulders.

"Listen, no matter what happens, I want you to know that I'm here for you."

He nods and takes another sip of his coffee.

I want to encourage him to stay strong and to tell him that everything is going to be okay.

But somehow, the words don't seem to come out right.

Nothing is quite hitting the spot.

"What are you going to do about Blake?" Aiden asks after a brief moment of silence.

That question catches me off guard.

"I don't know what you mean."

"I don't even know why it didn't occur to me to call the police earlier," he says quietly. "And I'm sorry about that. But it's not too late."

"What? Call the police?"

The thought had never crossed my mind.

"Ellie, he tried to rape you. I mean, you stopped him, but if I hadn't come in and you hadn't fought so hard...I can't even fathom that."

I shrug and look away.

"All I am trying to say is that if you want to press charges, I'm here for you."

"I don't know," I say after a moment. "I mean, everything turned out fine. Do you want me to press charges?"

I search his face for the answer.

I can't tell if he wants me to go to the police and won't actually come out and say it, but his expression is difficult to read.

It's too full of fury and anger.

"It's not up to me."

"I know that. I'm just asking."

"Well, you shouldn't."

"Why?"

"Because it's not fair," he says quietly. I don't really understand what he means by that.

"The thing is that if I go to the cops then I will have to tell them everything that happened on the yacht. I mean, I'd have to tell them about the auction, right?"

He nods, hanging his head.

"But that's not something that you want everyone to know about, right? I mean, like your investors?"

Aiden looks up. His piercing gaze cuts me to the very soul.

"It doesn't matter what I want, Ellie. Don't you get that? I mean, this isn't about me. It's about doing what's right for you."

My mind goes through a million different iterations of how this can go if I go to the police. And all of them come to the same conclusion.

"Listen, everything turned out fine. I got him off me and you really took care of him. And if I were to go to the police now, all of this stuff would become public knowledge. I mean, you're a pretty famous person. And even if you weren't, an auction on a yacht is a pretty big deal. It would drive away the investors that are still with you. And you definitely wouldn't be able to recruit anyone new to try to save the company."

Aiden is staring into space somewhere behind me. I wait for him to say something.

"I don't want you to not get justice just for my sake," he says quietly. "I mean, we should've called them when it first happened. It's not right."

I nod in agreement.

"I don't want everyone to find out about the auction. And it's not just for you. I'm not really sure I want my parents to know that I did that. I mean, it would become fodder for all the gossip magazines and I'm kind of a private person."

"All I want to reiterate is that I don't think you should take me or Owl into consideration in this decision. What Blake did was wrong and I won't stop you or even try to dissuade you from going to the cops or going public with it, if that's what you want to do. The wrong was committed against you. So, you have to decide for yourself."

I stare at him, dumbfounded.

"But how can I possibly make that decision without taking you into consideration, Aiden?" I ask. "I mean, I love you. And you're part of my life. A big part."

"I am?" he asks.

I nod.

"I love you, too. I just don't want you to—"

I put my index finger over his mouth. We are going in circles and one of us has to put a stop to it.

"I'm not going to go to the police," I say decidedly. "I don't really want the fact that I participated in the auction to become public knowledge and I'm glad that we stopped whatever was going to happen with Blake from going any further. So, I don't want to press any charges."

Aiden nods.

He would never admit it, but I see that he's relieved.

Going to the cops would put his company into an even more of a precarious situation and I don't want to hurt him anymore than he is already being hurt.

He's in the process of losing everything that he has worked for his entire adult life.

"So, what are your plans now?" I ask.

"In terms of what?"

"Owl?"

Aiden inhales deeply.

It's morning and another work day has begun. And staying cooped up from the rest of the world is probably not the wisest decision.

"I don't really know," he says, sighing. "I guess I'm going to call the rest of the investors and try to convince them to stay with me, despite the fact that the price of the company's stock is in free fall. And then, I guess I'll call my lawyers and try to figure out the total damage."

"That sounds like a good plan."

"I have a few that aren't exactly Blake's best friends, so I hope that they hang in there with me for a while longer. Hopefully, they haven't given up on me yet."

CHAPTER 13 - ELLIE

*D*espite his raging hangover, Aiden got on the phone soon after and I show myself out.

Aiden has a lot of work to take care of, and no longer plagued by insecurities about where we stood in our relationship, I feel inspired and excited to get back to my own writing.

I sit down in front of my laptop as soon as I got home, without even bothering to change into something more comfortable.

When I was little, my mom taught me to change into my comfy home clothes as soon as I got home.

It was mainly to keep my outside clothes looking nice, but I kept up the tradition when I got older.

That's why, even now, you'd never find me in a pair of skinny jeans or boots or even a bra at home.

No, when I'm home, I'm always in my pajamas.

They aren't the fancy matching kind like the ones they sell at Victoria's Secret.

No, they're just a pair of sweats or yoga pants or elephant pants and a loose fitting long-sleeve shirt, since I'm almost always cold.

Oh, yeah, and I always take off my bra and shoes whenever I get home.

That is except for today. I pull off my boots under the table while my laptop boots up, take a sip from the bottle of water I left on my desk the last time I was here, and open up my book.

I scan the last bit, and then quickly type up a paragraph of what's going to happen in the next chapter. Then I set a timer on my phone and start typing.

The timer is something I read about in a book by Rachel Abbott, *From 2k to 10k*.

It includes a number of strategies that she uses to start writing more words during the day.

When I was in college, the idea of writing two thousand words in a day seemed like a lot.

But Rachel regularly clears eight to ten thousand!

Her results are nothing if not inspiring and, ever since I've read that book, I've been implementing her approach to great success.

Timing your writing is one of her strong points. Just set the timer and write as much as you can in a particular interval of time.

Twenty minutes is my favorite.

It's short enough to summon a burst of energy, but long enough to actually produce real word count.

Well, as soon as I start the timer, I lose myself in the story and the twenty minutes flies by.

Since I'm in the middle of an exciting chapter, I restart it again and continue to type furiously.

Six sessions or two hours later, I go through my session and am pleasantly shocked by my productivity.

I have averaged about seven hundred words per session and come up with forty-five hundred words toward my final manuscript!

"Holy shit!" I exclaim.

Fueled by some mystical combination of coffee, momentum, and excitement, I press on.

The story is just getting good, meaning that I'm about to write a very juicy sex scene and I don't want to put it off.

The rest of the day proceeds at the same frantic pace. I lose myself in my writing, in a manner that was previously unfamiliar to me.

I'm so excited by what I'm writing and, to tell you the truth, aroused as well, that the words just appear on the page without much effort.

It seems like as long as I keep my butt in my seat, the story keeps telling itself without much input from me.

It helps a lot that it's something that I've just experienced and lived through. Though I do take the opportunity to embellish it somewhat.

How does that saying go again?

Never let the truth get in the way of a good story. Well, I believe in that wholeheartedly.

When twilight closes in on my window and the city lights up for the night, I type The End.

I stare at the cursor for a while, lost in thought.

Wow, I actually finished it.

I have completed a novel.

This might not be a big deal for many people, but for me, it is revolutionary.

I'm the person who struggled to write a two-thousand-word short story.

So, the idea that I actually completed a fifty-seven-thousand-word novel is breathtaking.

I don't think I've ever been so proud of myself before.

There is, of course, still a lot of work to do.

I need to re-read it and edit it for mistakes and typos and better word choices.

But now is not the time for that. Now, is the time to celebrate the fact that I'm done with my first draft!

I save my manuscript three times, to both my desktop and iCloud, to make sure that nothing is going to happen to it, and head to the kitchen.

Suddenly, it occurs to me that I've written for hours without taking a break or having a bite to eat.

As I pour myself a generous glass of red wine, some fancy brand that Caroline probably paid way too much money for in one of those little boutique grocery stores that she loves to patronize, I change into my favorite pair of elephant pants.

They are those harem pants with elastic on the bottom of each ankle, but they are incredibly soft and comfortable and have bright elephants on them.

How I managed to get all that writing done without wearing these is beyond me.

I take a big gulp of wine, without bothering to smell it first, and embrace the tartness as it runs down the back of my throat.

Somewhere between my first and second glass of wine while mindlessly flipping through the DVR recordings and trying to decide what I should watch, the title for my book pops into my head.

Auctioned Off.

Yes, perfect.

That's what I'm going to call it.

I scroll through the Amazon romance section on my phone, looking at the covers and the authors. Ever since I decided to write this book,

I've read a number of the titles and some of the authors have come out with additional books. Wow, these women write fast.

I look at the publication dates of one of my favorite ones and see that she publishes a book every month. And I thought I was productive, I think to myself, shaking my head.

Okay, in addition to the title, I also need a new name. I can't very well publish this under my own since I'm still on the fence about whether I want my mom to read it, let alone my other less understandable family members.

A pseudonym will give me privacy and with privacy I will have the freedom to write more books like this without worrying about Tom or my old colleagues at BuzzPost or even Caroline, for that matter, disapproving.

Not that I really care what they think.

Except that I do.

This book is full of truth and full of sex, and it's not something that I necessarily want everyone I went to high school with to know about me.

Okay, I got it.

Ella because it's pretty close to Ellie, but not exactly the same.

And for my last name?

How about Montgomery?

Yes, that's it! Ella Montgomery.

I've always loved the way these long Southern last names just roll off the tongue.

Well, maybe this is my opportunity to give myself a little bit of that.

With a title and an author name, I'm nearly halfway there.

Now, all I need is a cover.

Of course, that's a bit more complicated.

I scroll through the covers on Amazon with an eye for details.

A photo of a really hot guy with an amazing body seems to be a necessity.

But everything else?

Hmm, maybe it's something I can do myself as well.

I mean, I did take a Photoshop class that one summer in college. I can always hire someone, but maybe I should at least sketch it up first so I have some idea of what I want.

A few hours later, long after I finish the bottle of wine, I am done with a good mockup of the cover for *Auctioned Off*, Ella Montgomery's first novel.

The stock image of the guy with amazing pectoral muscles and a ripped six pack is definitely the selling point, but my manipulations and combinations of different fonts for the title and the author name are definitely eye-pleasing. I guess that Photoshop class wasn't a waste of time after all.

Okay, that's enough for tonight, I decide. But before turning off the computer, I go into various romance book groups that I've joined and ask for recommendations for editors.

Tomorrow, with a less alcohol-induced outlook, I will re-read my book and review the cover. My only hope is that they will both live up to the opinion that I have of them tonight.

As I climb into bed, my phone vibrates. I look at the screen.

I love you, Aiden texts. My heart immediately skips a beat and gives me butterflies.

I love you, too. I text back.

CHAPTER 14 - AIDEN

WHEN IT STARTS TO RAIN...

*T*he more time that I spend with Ellie, the more power I feel her have over me. I don't really mean it in a bad way, but it's definitely disarming.

I'm not someone who gives up power easily. I've never given it up to my ex-wife, and she was the last woman who even got close enough to challenge it.

But maybe using the word 'power' isn't the right thing. Ellie and I aren't on opposite sides of a war. We're not in competition.

No, what we have is actually the complete opposite of anything like that. Still, I find myself unable to think about anything else but her.

I crave her.

I want to have her.

I want to spend every waking moment with her.

And that's where the essence of her power comes in. I love the way she refuses to compromise and always stands her ground.

I love the way that she challenges me, pushing my boundaries. She's unlike any other woman I've ever met. Sitting here, looking out of the window onto the whole of New York below, my heart seizes up for a moment.

It skips a beat when a terrifying thought pops into my head.

What if I were to lose her?

Could I actually move on with my life?

There is no answer to this.

All I see and feel within my heart is darkness.

And if this isn't power, the most powerful force that one person can have over another person, what is?

It begins to rain and the charms of early fall with all of its golden leaves and dry, crisp weather turns into the dreariness of late October.

I hate to admit it, but weather has a big effect on my mood. The dark clouds and overcast skies without a single ray of sunshine make me feel melancholy and displaced.

Since the holidays are coming up and the dog days of summer are not so far behind us yet, the city is still filled with some levity and brightness.

But once the New Year comes and goes, and the dark days of winter set in with their black slush that once used to be snow, my heart really starts to ache for another type of life.

I watch as thick, proud raindrops pound against my floor to ceiling windows. They make me feel cold inside, even though I have the heat up enough to wear a t-shirt inside if I wish.

I would never admit this out loud to anyone, except maybe Ellie, but one of the main reasons that I love being as wealthy as I am now is that I never have to be cold in the winter if I don't want to.

Growing up, my mom was a total thermostat freak. Of course she had to be this way, because propane gas isn't cheap and the winters in New England are long and cold. She didn't make much money and we saved where we could.

We never bought brand foods, for one, or many fruits and vegetables. Instead, I subsisted on mainly only store brands and foods with very little nutritional value. I didn't mind this much, even though I know now that it was all junk food.

A lot of processed foods with white flour, canola oil, and refined sugars. But this isn't what bothered me most about my childhood.

It was the cold.

Most of the houses we lived in were very poorly insulated with single pane windows, and mom never turned the heat up enough. It was often in the mid-60s inside in February when the temperatures often dropped into the teens and twenties.

So, as you can imagine, single pane windows and poor insulation were not enough to keep us cozy.

Come to think of it, I don't really know if Mom was just never really cold herself or just used to always wearing three sweaters inside the house.

All I know is that there were many nights that I

spent wearing gloves inside the house because otherwise my hands would turn to icicles typing against the keyboard.

So, when I got older and got rich, the one thing that I have never denied myself is adequate heating.

If I want the house, or the apartment, or my office to be in the mid-70s in the middle of winter, so be it. They are my bills and I don't mind paying them.

Perhaps it's a silly thing to complain about something like heat when there are people out there with really terrible childhoods, but that's the thing about people, isn't it?

It's hard for us to relate to others because the problems that we have always appear much larger than other people's issues.

In other words, it's a bigger deal if we fall down and sprain our ankle than if a person in another country, across the ocean, gets blown up by a bomb.

———

THE DREARINESS OUTSIDE makes me feel cold, sending shivers up my spine. I turn up the

thermostat and turn on the kettle to make
some tea.

I know that it's not just the weather that's putting me
into a melancholy mood, and I stop fighting the
thoughts that try to creep in around the edges.

These thoughts are dark, full of anger, and distrust.
I've been trying to push them away for days and have
been mildly successful as long as the television
was on.

But distractions only work for a period of time. One
moment, it just all gets too much and no matter how
much you try to keep the world at bay, it comes
flooding in.

The first thought comes in a flash, just as the kettle
shuts off automatically after boiling the water.

I hear Ellie yelling for help through the door. We're
back on the yacht. I'm in the hallway, about to knock.
I'm excited to see her, my cock is hard with
anticipation. But all of the feelings of how that night
is going to go vanish, the moment that I hear her
screaming "Help!"

There is somebody there with her, I remember
thinking.

But why?

How?

She's supposed to be there alone. As these thoughts swirl around in my head, I don't let them distract me from the task at hand. I burst in through the door and run across the room. A few moments later, I'm on top of him.

It takes me a few punches to even recognize the person that I'm punching. His face flashes before my eyes as we tussle on the floor. Blake is taller than I am and has a good ten or twenty pounds on me.

His weight is a definite advantage and he gets a few blows in. My head starts to pound. I taste something metallic and warm in my mouth.

It's blood, probably mine.

This makes me angry.

I use the spark of anger to pin his arms under my knees and punch him over and over again in his face until someone pulls me off him.

If those security guards hadn't come in right there and then, I don't think I would've had enough strength within me to stop.

All I saw were flashes of black and red and the only thing I had on my mind at that moment was what I saw him doing, or trying to do, to Ellie.

The last time that I'd been in a fight, before Blake, was in middle school.

I'm not a fighter.

I'm more of a pacifist.

I don't like confrontations, especially physical ones. I don't thrive on conflict and competition.

All of that is a game that I play with other men who are my competitors in business. That's why I actually enjoy working with women more. They are kinder and more cooperative. They don't see the world as a zero-sum game.

They don't think that if one person is winning, then someone else out there is necessarily losing. And I don't think that way either. I believe that in business, and in life, we are all much better off if we work together for the greater good.

But these are not popular opinions to have, especially for a CEO. There are just way too many old men in positions of power who believe that the world owes them something. And it's not just old men. Blake isn't old, but he definitely believes this as well.

I've known Blake for a very long time. He invested in my company, Owl, back when it was just a spark of an idea.

It not only didn't have any sales, it was about a hundred years away from being pre-revenue, a fancy way of telling potential investors why they are putting money into a company that's producing no returns.

But I'm under no illusions as why to Blake Garrison invested in Owl, even back then. He came from a very well-off family who own forty percent of the Maine coastline.

They started in timber back in the nineteenth century and then evolved with the times, investing in whatever was the business of the future and would make them the most on their investment.

When we met at Yale, Blake was a fun guy who knew how to throw a good party and get all the girls to come. He had skills that I never had, in that department, especially.

But when it came to school, Blake was pretty useless. He didn't understand the first thing about coding. He couldn't solve an ordinary differential equation to save his life.

Yet, he had a hunch. He knew that I could do these things and he believed in Owl when I first described the idea to him.

It was his and his father's investment that allowed me to actually start the company and devote all of my energy to it. And as a result, they own a very substantial portion of it. But beyond their own share, there are other concerns.

They are the ones that brought in most of the other investors. These people aren't my friends, and they never want to be my friends. They want me to make them money, but that's where our relationship ends.

And, unfortunately, right now, Owl is free to use and doesn't really generate any money.

I have plans to invest heavily in an advertising platform, similar to what Google and Facebook have, and monetize the company that way.

Blake was always on board with this approach and I thought that we were on the same page. But after that night with Ellie, everything went to hell in a hand basket.

He's acting like he doesn't care about Owl anymore, or his investment. He only wants me gone. And the rate that everyone is pulling out, it's not that unlikely of a proposition.

As the rain continues to pound on my windows, I drop a mint tea bag into a cup of boiling of water and watch as it floats to the top, gets heavy with water, and eventually drops down below the surface.

"Fuck you, Blake," I whisper.

I feel my blood boiling below the surface as it courses through my veins. The anger that I have toward him acts on many different levels at once and I have a hard time differentiating one from the other.

First and foremost, I'm angry at him for assaulting Ellie. I'm angry that he dared to scare her.

I'm angry that he took it so far and that it required me physically overpowering him to stop.

I'm also angry at myself for not knowing this about him. I mean, I've been working with this guy for years.

How the hell did I not know that he was the type who was capable of raping a woman, or attempting to rape her?

He was toying with her.

He was getting off on scaring her.

I clench my fist and jaw at the thought of that.

And then, of course, my anger exists simultaneously on other levels as well. I'm angry at letting him get so involved in my company that he could have so much power over me now. I'm also angry at myself for not building my own relationships with our investors and just relying on him to do all the hard work.

Relationships have never been my strong suit, but I'm the fucking founder and CEO of one of the biggest tech companies in the world.

How could I let everything that I've worked for be compromised like this? What the hell was I thinking?

I look down at my phone.

My lawyers and business managers, and a million other people, have been calling me non-stop. Most just call with questions, offering very little in the way of answers in return. I don't know what to do about any of this.

One of the lawyers actually suggested that I apologize to Blake and invite him back to the negotiation table.

Me?

Apologize?

He had to be kidding, right?

I did nothing wrong.

And Blake is, frankly, lucky that Ellie is refusing to press charges against him.

It's really against my own counsel and better judgment, but I know that she's doing it for me.

I clench my fists again and watch how the blood drains from my hands, turning my knuckles white. There's that anger again.

I want Ellie to tell the cops what happened, but I also don't want that. If she goes to the police, then she will have to tell them about my yacht party and the auction.

If investors are running from me now, they will

definitely flee when they hear that I'm auctioning women off to the highest bidder on my yacht. Even if they are giving their consent.

No, Ellie is right not to go to the police, but I hate myself for it because I know that she's doing it to protect me. And I both hate and love her for it.

I take a deep breath. I listen to the way that my heartbeat starts to hurry without my control or consent. My head starts to feel cloudy.

And then...there's me feeling powerless again, even though I'm one of the richest people in the world.

Well, not anymore, but at least according to the last issue of Fortune Magazine.

Ha, isn't that funny?

I laugh out loud. I don't know exactly how much money I've lost, but it's somewhere over a billion dollars.

That's a lot of money. I know that. Of course, I know that. But you shouldn't feel bad for me. Haven't you ever heard that saying, don't ever feel bad for a man with his own plane?

Well, I stand by it.

I've been poor and I've been rich.

Being rich is definitely better, but at least I had a billion dollars to lose, right?

Besides, this is America.

Families are always rising and falling in America.

A big part of me thinks that you're not doing it right if you're not.

It's just money after all.

It's nice to have, but it's the journey that's important, not the destination.

CHAPTER 15 - ELLIE

WHEN I WAKE UP WITH A HANGOVER…

*C*aroline bursts into my room, waking me as if from the dead. I don't know what time it is, but the sun is shining through the windows and New York is full of bustle and activity below.

"I can't find my striped, crew neck, long sleeve shirt," Caroline says, helping herself through my closet. "Taylor and I are going to the zoo."

It takes me a good minute to remember who the hell Taylor is. Through the thick fog of the huge hangover, which makes my blood feel like molasses coursing through my veins, it finally hits me. Taylor is the guy she met on Aiden's yacht. He's the one who bought her at the auction.

"What is he doing here?" I ask. My mouth is parched and I cough in the middle of the question. When I sit up in bed, my body feels broken. Every inch of it aches and I wince in pain. My body is in full regretful mode from my drinking last night.

"Ah, of course, here it is!" Caroline yells. Her peppiness and natural zest for life is particularly annoying to me at this moment. The other thing that really aggravates me is the fact that she can party all night, drink way more than she should, and subsist on only a few hours of sleep without much effort. I, on the other hand, need a full eight hours or more just to not feel like a zombie most of the day.

"Honestly, I don't know how you sleep so much," Caroline comments, as if she's able to hear my thoughts.

She stands in front of my floor-length mirror and places the shirt against her shoulders. She's dressed in an elegant silk bathrobe with faux fur trim, which makes her look like a movie star from the 1950s. I'm not sure what she's wearing underneath, but I wouldn't be surprised if it were one of her elegant, lacy nightgowns. Following her lead, I got myself one of those when we first moved in together so that I could feel like more of a grown up, but it never felt right. I never could sleep in it straight through the night because of its tiny spaghetti straps and the lace that made me itch as I tossed and turned. So, I reverted to wearing old t-shirts and mismatched pajama pants.

"I've been looking for this shirt forever," she says, taking off her bathrobe and nightgown and pulling it over her bare breasts. Caroline isn't exactly the type of girl to burn her bra, but she's also not one who's shy about going out with her nipples hanging out. And why should she be? She has large breasts with perky little nipples that always stand up straight on their own and seem impervious to gravity.

"I'm sorry about that," I mumble. "I honestly can't remember the last time I even wore it."

"Oh, man, you are hungover," Caroline announces the most obvious thing in the world. I nod. If I had any more energy, I would ask her to pull the curtains closed and leave me to suffer alone in my dark room. Unfortunately, I don't even have the strength to do that.

Caroline walks over to my desk and picks up the empty bottle of wine.

"Wow, you had yourself a little party last night, didn't you?" she asks. I nod. My laptop is still open on the table and the pages of notes are laying around all over the place.

"Is this your new book?"

I nod. She knows that I'm working on a romance novel, but not really much else about it.

"I actually finished it last night," I say. "And got the cover done. And sent it to a proofreader."

"Oh, wow, that's awesome. This is the fastest you've ever written anything, right?"

Caroline is well aware of the fact that it used to take me weeks to squeeze out a 2,000 word short story.

"Yeah, I actually managed to write fifty five thousand words in about fifteen days," I say proudly. "I don't really know how, but they just came out of me. It was like I was possessed and someone else was doing all the hard work for me."

"Is that what they call a muse?" Caroline asks.

"History is full of stories about writers and their muses and the great lengths they go to just to hold onto their muses. I mean, the Greeks were practically obsessed with them."

I never really thought of it that way before, but she's right. Of course, I know about muses. I even did a paper on them my sophomore year. The muses are inspirational goddesses of literature, science, and arts in Greek mythology. They are considered the main source of knowledge that comes from poetry, songs, and myths and they were later adopted by Roman culture from the Greeks. Ancient authors would invoke a muse when writing epic histories and poetry and ask for inspiration and help from the muses. Ancient texts are famous for how much credit they are given by their creators and they are attributed in Homer's The Odyssey, Virgil's the Aeneid, and Dante's Inferno. They even come into play in later literature including those by Chaucer, Shakespeare, and Milton. In modern times, the concept of the muse typically refers to a real person who inspires the writer, musician, or artist to create her work.

"So, what's this book about?" Caroline asks, sitting

down at my desk and turning on my laptop. She doesn't hide the fact that she's a big snoop and I don't really mind it.

"Wow, I love the cover," she says, looking at the image in Photoshop that I created last night. "Auctioned Off. An alpha billionaire romance by Ella Montgomery."

Hearing the title of my book being read out loud sends shivers through my body. I watch her click over to the Pages document and read the blurb at the top.

"Oh my God, Ellie!" Caroline screeches. "This is about the yacht. And Aiden."

"Yes, I know." I shrug.

"Is it like, exactly what happened?"

"Yep, pretty much. I think that's why I was able to write it so quickly. Because it was pretty much true. I just wrote down everything that happened the first time I was there."

"Oh my God! Can I read it? Of course, I can read it, right? You're going to post it on Amazon," she says.

Without even waiting for me to reply, she sends the document to her email.

"Yes, it's fine," I agree, even though my permission is clearly not needed.

But in truth, I do want her to read it. She would be my first real reader. And, given what I know about Caroline, I know that she won't be a very harsh critic. Even though she has an Ivy League education, she isn't one to put her nose up at popular culture. She loves Supernatural, Vampire Diaries, and Pretty Little Liars, and has a somewhat unhealthy relationship with teen melodramas. Plus, she actually reads romance novels. She read *Fifty Shades of Grey* even before it was published by the big name publisher and became mommy porn across America. And she will definitely not be turned off by the explicit nature of my book either. Her philosophy is that the more hot sex that a book has, the better it is.

Suddenly, an unfamiliar, sickening feeling throws my body into a cold sweat. My hands start to shake and my stomach starts to rumble. Before I even know what's going on, I run to the bathroom. I barely have enough time to open the lid before an avalanche of vomit comes pouring out of my mouth.

I continue to throw up and shake until I empty every last bit of my stomach contents. It takes me a few moments to realize that Caroline is standing next to me on the tile floor, holding my hair out of my face. I've been in this position with her a number of times and it makes me feel good that she's here for me now.

"Okay, I'm really excited that you finished your book and all," Caroline says, "and the fact that Aiden Black is your muse, but don't you think it's funny that you're starting off your new career with your head in the toilet?"

I wipe my mouth with the back of my hand and force a smile. She helps me onto my feet and I brush my teeth harder and with more toothpaste than I ever have before.

"You think Aiden is my muse?" I ask.

"Of course!" Caroline says. "How else would you be able to get all that writing done so quickly?"

I mull that over for a moment. Yes, I guess she's right.

He is my inspiration for all of this. Without him and my experience on the yacht, I wouldn't have much to write about at all. Plus, to tell the truth, I'm kind of a prude. I don't like talking about sex, let alone sharing my sex life with the world. And yet, Auctioned Off is practically all sex. Unapologetic, hot, explicit, and dirty. But also loving. Because that's what Aiden and I have.

***

I get out of bed slowly, trying rather unsuccessfully to steady myself on my feet. The whole room spins all around me.

"I swear to God. I will never drink again," I mumble, leaning against a chair to make sure that I don't fall down.

"Oh, c'mon." Caroline laughs. "There's no need to be so rash. Besides, as a writer, you'll be in great company as a drunk."

"What do you mean?"

"Well, you know, all of these great men writers everyone always talks about from history. They were major drunks!"

My mind wanders back to my English major courses, but not a single name pops into my head.

Caroline helps me out. "Hemingway? Faulkner? Jack London?"

"Oh, yes, of course. Famous drunks."

"Almost as famous for drinking as they were for writing," she says.

"Oh, yeah," I add. "Wasn't it Hemingway who said that you should always write drunk and edit sober?"

"Sounds about right." Caroline laughs. "Well, listen, I'm going to leave you here to recover a bit. Because I have a breakfast date with Taylor."

"You do?"

"Yep!"

"Did he sleep over here?" I ask.

She nods and jumps up a little bit with excitement.

"Talk about burying the lead. So, what was it like?"

"Really fun," she says. "Really great. I like him, Ellie. A lot."

By the expression on her face, I can immediately tell that there's isn't an ounce of a lie in that statement.

"Well, say hi to him for me," I say.

"You don't want to come out and do the honors yourself?"

I shrug. "I feel like crap," I sigh. "Maybe another time."

CHAPTER 16 - ELLIE

I'm not a particularly vain person, but I don't like to make a habit of talking to attractive, hot men without taking a shower first and at least changing out of my pajamas.

Caroline shrugs and tosses her hair before leaving the room. I hear them talking out in the hallway as I sit down at my desk. I stare out of the window at the foggy, fall New York morning outside. Most of the leaves in the city have fallen, leaving the trees barren and naked. This time of year always makes me very sad. The holidays are still pretty far away and none of the lights and other decorations are up yet. In this moment, the city seems to just sit in wait, in anticipation of something bigger.

As large, voluptuous rain drops hit the glass, I turn

my attention to my laptop and scroll through my emails. Surprisingly, the proofreader came back with an edited manuscript.

ELLIE,

I couldn't put this book down. I was sick with a cold last night, but decided to open it and just take a look. Two hours later, I was done! It's awesome. Thank you so much for taking me away from my misery for a few short hours.

Kora

I DON'T QUITE BELIEVE what I've just read, so I read it again. And again. Is she for real? Wow, I never knew that my writing could have such an impact. My heart fills with joy. I have to tell someone. I want to reach out to my mom, am about to dial, but then realize that it's too soon to tell her. No, I don't want this to become some negative experience in case she comes down on me about writing romance novels in the first place.

I pick up the phone and text Aiden. I send him a

screenshot of what the proofreader said. He writes back within a few moments.

Wow, Ellie! That's great news. I'm so proud of you!

I GET up to pace around the room. Glancing at myself in the mirror, I look past the pale skin, the dark circles under my eyes, the messed up hair, and the tattered clothes that are only modestly passing for pajamas. Instead, all I see is the smile that won't go away.

After taking a shower and writing back to the proofreader, I accept all the changes that she's made to the manuscript - mainly fixing typos and little inconsistencies - and try to think of what to do next.

Self-publishing isn't like normal publishing. It's not just submitting a book to an agent or a publisher and letting them do all the heavy lifting. I'm not an expert, but I have been listening to a ton of podcasts and reading a bunch of blogs that talk about the different ways to approach this. One thing that is for sure, I need to start a mailing list. And the best way to get people to subscribe is to give away the book for free in exchange for an email address.

I format the Pages file of text into a mobi file for Kindle as well as an ePub file and attach the cover. Then I go to Bookfunnel and Instafreebie, open accounts, and upload my book. I then sign up for Mailerlite, where I get the first one thousand subscribers for free and connect the Bookfunnel and Instafreebie accounts to my Mailerlite account. I lie down on the bed and scroll through the Facebook groups that I recently joined with my new Ella Montgomery account. Many of these deal exclusively with Bookfunnel and Instafreebie giveaways of books for hungry and voracious readers. I fill out the forms and sign up for five in the coming month.

A few hours later, I'm even prouder of myself than I was when I received the email from the proofreader. I'm not a particularly techie person. Setting up all of these accounts and connecting them all to each other may not seem like a big deal to other people, but it felt insurmountable to me.

When I'm done, I want to reach out to Aiden again to tell him everything I managed to accomplish despite my horrible hangover, but my stomach growls. No, I need to get something to eat first. I head to the kitchen, hoping that I've given Caroline and Taylor enough time to get on with their breakfast plans. I'm pleased to discover that my apartment is completely deserted. I take out some eggs from the fridge and grab a fork. I beat the eggs until they're all one color. Then I add some coconut milk, my secret ingredient to making my scrambled eggs very fluffy and slightly sweeter than they would be normally.

While I swirl around the spatula to make sure that the eggs get even fluffier when they cook on the skillet, I flip on the television. An aggressive guy is screaming out of the screen and a scroll of stock news and other numbers that mean nothing to me flash on the bottom of the screen. I'm pretty sure that neither Caroline nor I have ever turned on CNBC, the financial news channel, on our own accord. No, this must be Taylor's handiwork.

I'm about to change the channel when another talking head appears on the screen and the two of them start to discuss the downfall of Owl.

Wait, did I hear that right? The downfall of Owl? Aiden's company?

I turn up the volume, turn off the flame on the stove, and listen in carefully. My head starts to buzz when I hear that the company already lost more than a billion dollars in valuation and there's no sign that it won't continue to lose money as the days proceed. The two talking heads argue over what the company should do and decide that getting rid of the CEO, Aiden Black, is the only way to salvage this mess that he's made.

I drop the remote control and it falls to the floor with a loud boom. Get rid of Aiden? Can they even do that? Isn't this his company?

As if they heard my questions in their studio, the two anchors announce that it is, of course, possible to get rid of the CEO. It's a public company and the CEO answers to a board of directors who make all the decisions. And if the board of directors isn't happy with something that the CEO is doing, they definitely have the power to kick him out for the greater good.

The greater good? The greater good of who? None of this is Aiden's fault. Blake pulled his money out of the company and talked a lot of trash about Aiden to other investors, causing an avalanche of people leaving Owl and taking their money with them. But how could they just believe him, just like that? Why didn't they give Aiden a chance to explain?

No, this can't be happening, I mutter to myself as my eggs grow colder and colder by the minute. I stare straight ahead unable to move a single bit of my body. My mind comes up with more questions than I can answer, leaving me in a state of immobilization. I can't manage to move a single muscle, let alone command myself to go to the kitchen and eat my breakfast. I feel completely useless.

My mind goes back and forth between whether or not I should call Aiden. On one hand, I want to tell him that I know what's going on. I want to tell him that I'm here for him. But on the other hand, I know that's just a lie. I mean, I am here for him, of course, but I don't really know what's going on. I'm only privy to second-hand information from a couple of people on television who are just speculating on what's going to happen. They know a little bit, but is it enough? He most definitely knows a lot more than the people on the financial news channel, who don't even seem like legit reporters, since they spent half an hour arguing about their positions.

Without fully deciding one way or another, I pick up the phone and dial. I don't know what I'm going to say when he answers; I'm just going to let the words flow out of me.

The phone rings once, twice, and a third time. Then it goes to his voice mail. He's not there. Either that or he's not answering on purpose.

A minute later, I receive a text, *I can't talk now.*

I decide to let the matter lie. There's nothing else I can do about any of this. I mean, if Aiden can't do anything, and neither can his minions of lawyers, what am I, a budding romance novelist, going to do?

CHAPTER 17 - ELLIE

WHEN I GO TO STRAND...

I look out of the window. The clouds are hanging low and the sky is dark even though it's barely noon. On days like this, I like to curl up with a good book in bed and keep the world and all of its problems an arm's length away. But something is different about today. As worried as I am about Aiden and his situation, I feel proud about what I have accomplished. It hasn't been that long since I decided to become a full-time author and here I am actually doing it. I'm actually facing all of my fears and insecurities. Don't get me wrong. They're still there in the back of my head. You know, all those thoughts that say that you're not good enough. That maybe you shouldn't even try. What's the fucking point? No one will like your work anyway. No, finishing this book was my way of saying a big fuck you to all of that. And I have to celebrate.

I head to my closet and pull on a pair of black tights, boots, and a sweater. I may not be a huge fan of cold weather, but at least it gives me the opportunity to get away with not wearing a bra without it being too obvious. I grab a light waterproof jacket and put a journal and my favorite Uni-ball vision pen into my purse. This isn't a work outing that's why I'm not bringing my computer. No, the journal is there only if inspiration strikes me.

In the hallway, I debate whether I should bring the umbrella as well and finally decide that I should. The jacket might be waterproof, but I don't want to start out this fall laying up in bed with the flu for a week because I got soaked everywhere else.

I slush my way through the New York City streets, avoiding eye contact with all the other poor souls who are out in this weather. Most are dog walkers, but there are also a few willing participants like I am. Finally, I reach 828 Broadway Avenue, right between 12th and 13th Streets. When I see the sign for the bookstore across the street, my heart fills with joy.

This is my happy place. Other people love bars and restaurants and malls, but I'd take a used bookstore any day of the week and twice on a Sunday. Strand Bookstore may be the largest bookstore in New York, if not on the East Coast. It definitely feels that way. It's a large labyrinth place that smells of tattered covers and much loved old books. They are famous for being so big, their tagline is that they sell books by the foot and that they have eighteen miles of books. The place has been around since 1927, which always makes me feel very privileged to have the opportunity to be here. I wander in between the aisles, briefly looking at the categories.

The thing is that what I love most about used bookstores is that, unlike regular chain stores like Barnes and Noble, you go in them never knowing what you're going to find. Their selection changes constantly as people donate and exchange their books for new books and a book that was here a few days ago may be gone today.

I head to the fiction section and then slowly make my way to the romance section. I look over the spines and run my fingers over the edges of the well-read books. People have loved these books dearly while they read them and then they let them go before moving on to another book.

Some people hold onto books forever; they keep every book they read. But I'm a pretty voracious reader and there's no way that I would ever have time for that. I've actually started reading a lot on my phone, downloading directly from Amazon. And as much as I love reading books on my phone, sometimes there's nothing like sitting on a couch with a cup of tea and a good book. Actually turning those pages that other people have turned - it makes me feel like I'm part of something bigger. Something that's not just bigger than I am, but that's bigger than all of us. I'm not a very religious person, but it makes my heart swell and makes me feel almost spiritual.

As I make my way aimlessly down the aisles, I pick up the books that look interesting to me, read the back covers, and feel them in my hands. I wonder what their writers are doing right now, at this very moment, and I wonder if they felt as excited as I did finishing their first novel. I really hope so. Otherwise, what would be the point?

Walking here through the aisles of books reminds me of the place that I worked in during the summer

between my ninth and tenth grade years in high
school. Now, I can't even remember what that place
was called and it was much smaller than the
Strand. It was probably around seven hundred
square feet of space, with every available space of
wall filled with books. That bookstore specialized
in genre fiction and they only carried used
romance, science fiction, fantasy, horror, and
thriller books. They also had a big book exchange
program where loyal customers could come back
and bring back the books they've read in exchange
for credit for new books. The group of old ladies
that always came in on Friday afternoons were
experts at the book exchange program and rarely
paid for any of their Nora Roberts and Danielle
Steel novels.

I hate to admit it, but when I was in high school, I
didn't really get them. In fact, I made fun of them. I
didn't think they were real readers. And by real, I
meant serious. But now, writing my first novel and
reading lots of romance novels myself, I realize that
everyone is a real reader. It doesn't really matter
what you read as long as you read. And it's more
often the case, that people who read genre fiction
that offers them some sort of escape, actually read a

lot more than those who read those so-called serious novels.

And that's all you can really ask for as a writer, isn't it? Someone who is willing to read your books voraciously and with great appetite. I wander back to the romance section and look over the piles of books that Danielle Steel has written and published. Her catalog is impressive, enough to make you think that there's no way you could ever write a third of these books in a lifetime. But then again, it's also inspirational. If she can do it, why can't I?

"Wow, well, I'll be damned," someone says behind me. The voice sounds familiar, but it takes a moment to realize who it belongs to.

"I never thought I'd catch you, of all people, with a Danielle Steel novel in her hands," Tom says.

CHAPTER 18 - ELLIE

Tom is one of my oldest friends. He and I were practically inseparable when we were in Yale and then things went all wrong. I was in love with him for close to two years, but it never felt like the right time to bring it up. And then he started dating Carrie Warrenhouse, of all people, the daughter of the owner of BuzzPost, the online magazine where we both got jobs after graduation.

"And what's wrong with Danielle Steel?" I ask.

"Um...what's wrong with Danielle Steel? Seriously?" Tom asks, furrowing his brows. He looks just as handsome and cocky as he always was, only this time, his demeanor and self-assuredness makes me feel nauseous.

"What are you doing here, Tom?" I ask.

"It's raining. I thought I'd head to the biggest used bookstore around. Probably same as you. New York is a small town if you're a writer," he says, leaning against a wall of books. I glance over at the book that he's carrying in his hand. It's Micheal Chabon's latest release. Micheal Chabon is the type of writer that is hailed by all the New York critics, but is not known to be a bestselling type of author. He's also Tom's hero.

"Yes, I guess so," I shrug and turn my attention to my book. If he's willing to just pretend that nothing happened between us last time, I'm definitely not.

"So, is this how it's going to be now?" he asks.

I shrug.

"I don't really know what you want me to say. I mean you said a lot of mean things to me last time."

"Yes, I know," he mumbles, hanging his head. "But you did, too."

I shrug. That's true as well.

"I wanted to call you after...but I didn't know what to say," he says carefully. "The thing is that Ellie, I just want to go back to how things were between us."

I look up at him. The look on his face definitely seems earnest. This is the look he gets when he's telling the truth. Despite everything, I know him well enough to know that.

Despite his earnestness right now, it is a little bit hard to forgive someone for calling you a whore. And the worst thing wasn't that he even called me a whore, but the fact that my friend called me that. I opened myself up to him, told him about what had happened on the yacht, and he made me feel very small and insignificant.

"Listen, I'm really sorry for everything I said," Tom says. "I really didn't mean to get so carried away. I was just...angry."

I resist the temptation to roll my eyes and wait for him to continue.

"I came over last time to tell you how I feel about you, and you just...pushed me away."

"So what? Didn't you think that could've been a possibility?"

"Of course, I knew you could reject me. That's what I was worried about," Tom says. "But still, I had hope, you know. I thought that everything would be okay. Somehow."

"It would've been if you hadn't made me feel so horrible after I told you about the auction."

Tom looks down at the floor. He takes a deep breath.

"I know. That was wrong. You should do whatever you want to do. I just felt rejected and I hated that feeling. And I'm sorry. I'm really, really sorry."

I take a deep breath. I'm not one to hold onto grudges for long, especially when people are genuinely sorry for what they have done.

"Okay," I say slowly. "I guess I can accept your apology."

"You can?" Tom's eyes light up. I nod slightly.

We stand in the aisle for a few moments, trying to figure out what to do next. There's always that awkward moment after one party forgives the other and you try to move forward, that you don't quite know what to do. I mean, you know that you need to start anew, but how to do that, exactly, alludes you. I look down at my feet and then at the Danielle Steel novel in my hand. A part of me is happy that I came here and ran into Tom. But another part just wishes I could spend the rainy afternoon curled up with a good book, keeping the real world away from me as far as possible.

"So..." I say after a moment. "What's going on with you and Carrie?"

Tom kicks his one foot with the other. He's wearing sneakers, which are muddy and probably soaking wet from slogging through the cold New York streets.

"She's good," he says. "We're good," he says quietly.

"Oh, that's good." I nod. My voice goes up a little when I say 'Oh' and I hope that he doesn't notice. I'm actually surprised that they're still together. The last time we spoke, it didn't seem like a relationship that he really wanted to be a part of anymore. And knowing Tom for as long as I have known him, I know that he's not the type to stick around if things are bad.

"You don't approve?" he asks, jokingly.

I shrug. "No, of course not. I mean, who am I not to approve?"

"One of my oldest friends."

I nod. That's true. We have been friends for a long time. A very long time. There was a time in my life when I didn't think that there was anyone else in the world who could know me as well as Tom does. And there was another time when I didn't think there was anyone else I wanted to let close enough to me to know as much as Tom did.

"So, the engagement is still on?" I ask.

"Yes." He nods. "Listen, that's another thing that I wanted to talk to you about. I'm really sorry for kissing you like that last time we talked. I don't really know what came over me the last time we spoke. It was stupid. Just some sort of nonsensical impulse. I love Carrie. I really do."

"I know that," I whisper. I nod and agree with him on everything that he says though, no matter how much he babbles on, tripping over his words, it's hard to believe any of it. His words say that he's sorry, but everything about the moment says that he's not sorry one bit. The only thing that he's sorry about is the fact that I pushed him away.

"Actually, I was going to call you, but since I ran into

you…I'd like to invite you to a get together that Carrie's parents are hosting for close friends and family. They have this cocktail party in the middle of early November as a way to bid farewell to the summer months and bring on the winter. They always have it before Thanksgiving and all the family holidays start."

"Wow, that sounds…fun."

"Yes, it is. Well, I've never been, but it should be fun. It's at their house in Maine."

"Oh," I say. I am speaking on monosyllables because I'm trying to think of whether I can still get out of this party or maybe it's something I should attend.

"In Maine?" I ask.

"Yes, they have this very large house, more like a compound, there, right on the water. They own like acres and it's not just one house, it has at least three or four guesthouses on the property."

"That sounds nice."

"They told me I can invite whomever, and I'd really like to invite you. And Caroline."

That's a new one for me. I know that there was never much love lost between him and Caroline.

"And if you want to bring your...guy friend...you're more than welcome to. You and Caroline both get plus ones."

"It sounds wonderful," I say after a moment. And then stop.

"But?" He fills in the words for me.

"Well, it just seems a little odd, I guess. I mean, you don't even like Caroline. And why would they want four people at the party who they don't really know?"

"That's sort of the point. The Warrenhouses are very friendly people and they love meeting new people. Especially those with connections. So, they told me to invite anyone I want. Especially, if I knew anyone from Yale."

I nod.

"And your guy friend...what does he do?"

We are both very well aware of the fact that he is deliberately not using the word boyfriend when referring to Aiden.

"He's in tech," I say coyly.

"And you said he owned a yacht? He must be doing very well."

I nod. "He's doing alright," I say.

"Well, bring him along. I know that Mr. Warrenhouse would love to meet him."

"And how do you know that?" I ask.

"Because he would love to meet anyone who owns a yacht."

When he says that, we both crack up laughing.

"So, is that why you want me to come?" I ask. "To be your buffer with her family."

"Um, yes, of course!" Tom says, smiling. "I'm terrified of her family. And the more people who can come who are my friends the better."

"Even Caroline?" I ask, skeptically.

"Yes, even Caroline." He caves. "Better to have the evil that I know than the one I don't."

I smile. "Well, when I pass on your invitation to her, I'll be sure to mention that you said that."

We both laugh again. It feels good to laugh with Tom. We used to be such great friends. We loved the same movies, books, and television shows. We could talk about everything. And then hormones and complicated relationship shit got in the way. Looking at him, laughing in front of me, I'm suddenly transported to freshman year at Yale and it feels like not a minute has elapsed since.

When we check out and Tom walks me to the door, the rain outside has dissipated and a few sun rays are peeking out from under the clouds.

"So, will you come?" Tom asks as we're about to say goodbye. "Please?"

"When is it?"

"In a few weekends. I'll send you all the details."

I nod. "You really want me to come?"

"Yes! Of course, I wouldn't ask if I didn't."

"Okay," I say tentatively. "I'll see what I can do."

"Great, that's all I ask. Perfect."

We stand for a moment, awkwardly unsure whether we should shake hands like perfect strangers or give each other a hug. Finally, we both decide to go for the hug and my world feels a slight bit lighter. Perhaps it is possible to be friends with a guy after all. Especially someone who has known you for as long as Tom has known me.

CHAPTER 19 - ELLIE

I walk home along the water-soaked streets with my head in the clouds. My bag is heavy with seven books that I purchased from Strand, but I haven't felt this light on my feet in a very long time. It's funny how you forget how someone used to make you feel until you come face to face with him again and are reminded in the bluntest way. I no longer have the romantic feelings that I used to have for Tom. Yet, all of those feelings seemed to have somehow been replaced with feelings of nostalgia and a longing for the past. C'mon, Ellie, you're too young to be nostalgic for the past, I say to myself crossing Broadway. You haven't been out of college for that many years. What are you going do when you're fifty, or seventy? Frankly, I don't really know. All I know is that there is a special place in my heart that's reserved just for Tom and it will likely always be there.

When I walk up to my building, I search my bag for my keys, trying hard to avoid plopping it on the dirty sidewalk. Instead, I crouch down, take out all the books that I've stuffed into it, and feverishly search for the keys that will undoubtedly be in the last place I look. The inanity of that statement is, of course, not lost on me as things you lose are always in the last place you look for them, mainly because you stop looking the moment that you find them, but still.

"Lost something?" a familiar voice says from above. I look up. Even though the sun is still behind the clouds, it is still very bright out and I have to squint to look up at the man standing above me. With the brightness of the clouds behind him, I can't make out his face, but I know exactly who it is.

"What are you doing here?" I ask with a big toothy smile on my face.

"I wanted to see you," Aiden says. "I also wanted to see your apartment."

"I have to warn you, we are not expecting visitors," I

say, standing up. My legs cramp up and it takes me a moment of hopping from one foot to another before I can take a step. Aiden watches me with amusement.

"It's okay. I don't mind messes," he says.

As we ride up the elevator, my whole body tenses up. This is the first time Aiden has ever been to my apartment. A big part of me wishes that he had given me some notice so I could actually clean up a little. The place is a total mess with clothes everywhere.

"It's okay that I came, right?" he asks. I look into his piercing eyes. I haven't seen him this vulnerable in a very long time. He is hurting inside and all of his pain is spilling out over the edges.

"Yes, of course!" I say, throwing my arms around him and giving him a kiss on the lips. I feel like he needs someone to take care of him in this moment, even though he won't admit it. And that's okay. I'm here for him.

"I'm just a little embarrassed over the state of my apartment. I had a little too much to drink."

"By the way, I'm looking forward to reading your book."

My heart clenches up. Oh my God. I can't believe this thought didn't even occur to me earlier. I mean, of course, he would want to read it. My face flushes red as I unlock my apartment. I try to hide my embarrassment by immediately starting to pick up dirty dishes from around the kitchen counter and throwing them in the sink.

Aiden walks into the living room and looks out of the big window, at the leafless trees below.

"You have a nice view," he says. I don't know if he's actually oblivious to my embarrassment or just lost in his own thoughts.

"Thanks. It's nice when there are leaves on the trees. But you know, it's October in New York."

"Yeah, it can get a bit dreary here, right?"

"Yep. Honestly, I thought I was the only one who noticed."

"Really?"

We watch as the drizzle outside turns back into big powerful rain drops, as if in an effort to prove our point.

"It's kind of funny that I've lived on the East Coast

my whole life, but I've never been a big fan of winters here. Or the spring for that matter," I say.

"Me either," Aiden says, turning to face me.

For a moment, I'm taken aback by how beautiful he is. His strong jawline accentuates his perfect lips and his slightly elongated nose is a perfect complement to his forehead. His dark hair is getting a little long, like he's a week or so overdue for a haircut, but I'm in love with the way it falls into his almond-shaped eyes.

"I think spring here is the worst. Unlike in Europe, where every day in March seems to get warmer and warmer, the weather here tends to oscillate between winter and summer. Some days are pretty warm and others, the wind blows in and it's as if we're never going to reach summer."

I smile.

"What?"

"I don't know," I say with a smile. "I never knew that you were such a big fan of warm weather."

He shrugs. "Yeah, I think I like the idea of snow. But the reality? Not so much. Would love to go sailing around the Caribbean and wear nothing but flip-flops all year round."

"I've never been to the Caribbean," I say. "I mean, I've been to South Florida, but not the islands. The sunsets there are magnificent."

"Yes, they are. So is the snorkeling and the diving," he says. "Maybe I'll have to take you there sometime."

That catches me off guard. I'd love that, of course, I would. But I never expected him to bring up going on a trip so soon into our relationship.

"What's wrong?" Aiden asks, taking a step closer to me.

"Nothing," I say, smiling. "Nothing at all. You saying that just makes me very happy."

As Aiden puts his arms around me, I suddenly feel safer than I have ever felt before. It's like he's a warm, luxurious blanket that engulfs me, protecting me from everything that's evil in the world.

When he presses his lips to mine, the muscles deep within me clench up in a delicious way. I had forgotten the electricity that somehow managed to surge through my body just with one look or kiss. The first kiss is merely a peck, but it quickly morphs into something more. His lips are slow and firm. They are demanding and strong. As they push and pull against mine, I feel him molding mine into what he wants them to be.

"I just wanted to tell you." Aiden pulls away slightly, keeping his eyes on me. I feel hypnotized, waiting for the next word that will come out of his beautiful mouth. "I still want to read your book. Just because we're doing this, that doesn't mean that I have forgotten about that."

Chills rush through my body. Aiden tugs at my sweater, kissing my neck and collarbone. Then he pulls it off my body with one swift motion. It takes me a moment to remember that I didn't put on a bra before I went to Strand. His eyes light up when he looks at my bare breasts. He even takes a moment to take a step back and admire the view. It doesn't last long enough to embarrass me, thank God.

"You are so gorgeous," Aiden whispers. "I don't know how I managed to forget how beautiful you are."

Now, I'm officially embarrassed. I feel my face flush and I try to look away. But he doesn't let me.

"I am going to tell you how beautiful you are over and over again," Aiden whispers. "Until you believe me. Until you know it to be the one true thing."

He is holding my cheeks, forcing me to focus my eyes on his, and I feel my cheeks getting hotter under his touch. Every time that I try to look away, he refuses to let me go. His piercing eyes look through me to my very core.

I give a little nod and he kisses me again. He buries his hands in my hair, grasping both sides of my head. It feels like he's cradling me, coaxing me. His hands slowly run down my neck and down my back as he presses me closer to him. He squeezes me tightly. Then one hand returns to the back of my head, pulling slightly on my hair, activating every strand with electricity. His other hand runs down my spine and toward the small of my back, hesitating slightly before going all the way down my butt. As I press against him, I feel his large erection pushing back against me, sending shivers up my body.

Before I can stop myself, I give out a moan. It's in the middle of a kiss and I feel like I'm moaning right into his mouth. I can barely contain myself, but the moan just turns him on even more. I want him. I want to pull off his clothes and plunge him deep within me, but I hold on and wait. Things are always better with a little anticipation, right?

Instead, I run my fingers over the outline of his strong biceps and the muscles that peek out from his shoulders. I move my hands up to his face, over his lips, and into his hair. His hair is soft and unruly, and my fingers get buried in each wave. As I curl my fingers slightly and tug his hair against his head, Aiden gives out a moan. His eyes roll to the back of his head with pleasure and I tug again. He groans again, eventually bringing his eyes back to meet mine.

"That feels really good," he says.

"I love burying my hands in your hair," I whisper.

Aiden bows his head for a moment before running his hands over my bare breasts. He presses my nipples in between his fingers slightly and now it's my turn to moan.

He pushes me back toward the couch until I feel it behind me. I'm about to lie down, but he props me back up. Instead, he drops to his knees in front me, grabbing my hips with both hands. A familiar warm

feeling starts to build at my very core as he licks his
lips and then pulls me toward him.

"You smell so good," he whispers.

"I want you," I mumble, enjoying the kisses.

He takes his time taking off my boots. I never knew
that having someone take off your shoes could be
so...sensual. But when it comes to my pants, he pulls
them and my panties off with one quick swoop.

Before I get a chance to even be embarrassed for
standing stark naked before him, Aiden stands up
and unzips his jeans. He unbuttons his shirt and
drops his jeans to the floor. He keeps his eyes on
mine as he removes his boxer briefs and then grabs
my hand.

"Where are we going?" I ask.

"Your bedroom. Which one is it?"

I point to my room and let him pull me toward my
bed. When we get there, he pushes me down on the
bed and pushes my legs apart with his body as he
squeezes himself in between my knees.

After kissing my neck and collarbone, he leans over
and kisses the inside of my thighs, creating a long

trail of kisses up and down my body. His lips travel up toward my belly and focus their attention on my navel. He continues his journey up, eventually pausing again at my nipple.

Pressing his hand around my other breast, he remarks, "you're a perfect fit for my hand."

My face flushes red as my breasts swell under his touch. My nipples get even harder than they were before. Aiden presses his lips around one nipple and pushes it gently between his teeth. I feel trapped and owned at the same time. The feeling sends electric impulses through my body. Every nerve ending in my body feels as if it's on fire.

"Aiden," I moan, tossing my head back.

Slowly, he sends his arm down my body, continuing to hold my nipple in his mouth. As soon as his fingers enter my body and make their way deep within me, I start to feel that warm sensation building somewhere in the pit of my stomach. My breathing speeds up. I grab a hold of his large erect cock and massage it in a slow manner.

"You're so wet," he whispers. "Oh, wow."

"And you're so hot," I say, speeding up my hand

motion a bit. Through his kisses, I hear him groan, moan, and start to lose control.

"I have to have you now," he moans and gets on top of me. I want him inside of me more than anything.

I spread my legs open for him and welcome him inside. He fills me up like I've never been filled up before. Or maybe I've just been feeling rather empty recently without him. Our breathing and movements match up as we start to move together in sync. My hips are his hips and my body is his body. I feel absolutely no separation between our two selves and it's the most natural thing in the world.

Suddenly, my throat tightens up as the warm sensation at my very core starts to build and build.

"I'm getting..." I don't get to finish saying that I'm getting close, before I give out a big powerful moan and surrender myself to him completely. Aiden continues to move inside of me for a few more moments before also reaching a climax.

"That was..." Aiden says, trying to catch his breath. "Amazing."

"Yes, it was." I nod. I'm keenly aware of the fact that I can't feel my legs and I don't care.

"I love you, Ellie," Aiden says without pulling out of me.

"I love you, too." I smile.

"I wish we could stay here forever."

"Me, too."

CHAPTER 20 - ELLIE

WHEN THINGS AREN'T EXACTLY WHAT THEY SEEM…

*L*ying next to Aiden after making love to him, I run my fingers over his perfectly sculpted chest and listen to his breaths. They are steady and calm. He breathes in with his nose and out with his mouth like they taught me in yoga class - the way that I couldn't quite get used to breathing in my everyday life.

"Well, that was a nice surprise," I say.

"Yes, and for me, too."

"Oh, c'mon, don't tell me that you didn't know what was going to happen."

He stretches his arms behind me, flashing a smile. "I had a hunch, but I wasn't sure. I mean, you can never be sure of these things, you know?"

I shake my head, not believing him for a second.

"But this isn't really why I came over," Aiden says.

"No?"

He shakes his head.

"I really missed you. I had to see you."

I love the sound of that.

"I missed you, too," I say.

It's still hard to believe that it's physically possible to miss someone you have just seen. I mean, up until a few weeks ago, I had no idea who Aiden Black was and I went about my life just fine. I actually thought I was doing okay. And now? Now, if I don't hear back from him throughout the day or don't see him, it feels like a part of me is missing. But now that he is in my life, all of my thoughts seem to focus entirely on him and what he is doing. I know that this may not be entirely healthy, but I don't really know what else to do with this insatiable need to be with him.

"I haven't felt like this in a very long time," Aiden says after a moment. "Actually, I don't think I've ever felt like this. It's strange to say, but it's like I'm obsessed with you, Ellie. I have to know what you're doing. I want to see you all the time."

"I know what you mean," I whisper.

"I just want to be with you all the time. It's like the world is a better place with you by my side."

I give him a small kiss on the lips and tell him that I feel the same way.

"Especially with everything that's going on with Owl," he adds. I look into his eyes. They are downcast and lacking in luster. The mere mention of his company, his life's work, and what's happening to it is enough to send him into a downward spiral of depression and sadness.

"I wanted to ask you about that," I say after a moment. I wait for him to continue, but he doesn't.

"I was watching CNBC..." I start.

"Oh, those assholes don't know anything."

"Okay, so what is going on?" I ask again. I want him to open up, tell me every last detail, but the mere thought of Owl seems to shut him down.

He looks away, somewhere past me, and then
gets up.

"Where are you going?" I ask.

Aiden pulls on his boxer briefs, then his pants, and
buttons up his shirt before turning back toward me.
He sits down on the bed. I clutch the bedspread
toward my bare shoulders and wait.

"It's all falling apart," he says after a moment. "Blake
is a lot more powerful and influential than I ever
thought he could be. I really underestimated him.
And the worst part? I don't know what to do about
any of it. I've called all the investors, practically
begging them to reconsider, but it was all to no avail.
He has convinced them and now they are happy to
lose a little bit of their investment rather than go
down with the whole company."

"Oh my God," I whisper.

"And the thing is that they don't have to lose much at
all. I mean, if they all decided to stay. But since
they're falling like dominos, there's not much I can
do to stop it. I need them all to suddenly change
their mind if I want to salvage any of the losses. But
I can't."

Aiden won't meet my eyes. Instead, he watches the rain pound against the window. I wish there were something I could do to help him. But I barely know what's going on. Then something occurs to me.

"Do you need money?" I ask.

"What?"

I repeat my question. I know that he will be tempted to lie, so I search his face for the truth.

"No, I don't need money," he says with half a chuckle.

"You gave me a lot of money, Aiden. Too much actually. So, if you need help…" I say with my voice drifting off at the end.

"First of all, I did not give you a lot of money."

"I made like thirty thousand a year at my job, Aiden. And after a night with you and then the week, I have more than I could ever spend."

"Okay, I know it was a lot of money for a regular person. But Owl has lost over a billion dollars already. Probably a lot more. A few hundred thousand won't make a big difference. And you know that, right? I mean, you have to know that."

I did know that. I mean, it's not like they lost a million dollars or even ten. A billion dollars is such an astronomical sum, I couldn't even begin to imagine how much that is. "So, what's going to happen now? Do you have any money saved?"

"I have no idea what's going to happen. I've never lost anything this big before. But my lawyers are already mentioning that I might have to step down for the good of the company."

"Step down?"

"The investors are pulling out because of me, so I might not have a choice if I want Owl to survive."

"Oh my God," I whisper. I put my hand on his shoulder, but he just brushes me off.

"It's all up in the air. No one really knows what's going on."

I don't know how to help him. I want to do something, but I can't think of anything. I mean, what can you do for someone in this position? Eventually, I coax him into having some tea with me. I've always been under the belief that tea has the ability to make everything okay, and if not totally okay, at least better. I toss of bag of mint tea into my cup and Aiden opts for a cup of English Breakfast. I find a box of sugar cookies in the back of the pantry and place those on the table as well. He barely takes a bite of his.

Sitting here, across from him, I feel completely helpless. And stupid. Mainly, I feel stupid because I actually thought that he was better. I mean, he came to see me and we had awesome sex. I thought that things were turning around for him. But he's actually just as distraught, if not more distraught, than he was before.

"I'm sorry, but I'm just so caught off guard by how messed up you are over Owl," I say and immediately regret the words that have just come out of my mouth. They sound so selfish and self-centered.

"What do you mean?" Aiden asks without seeming like he has taken any offense.

"It's stupid. I'm sorry I said anything."

"No, tell me."

"The last time I saw you, you were so fucked up. And when you came to see me this time, and we made love...I don't know, I just thought...that things were better."

He stares at me. At first, I think he's cross with me, but after a moment, a sly coy smile pops up at the corners of his mouth.

"Things aren't better," he says, shaking his head. "But making love to you did take my mind off them for a bit. And for that, I want to thank you."

"It did?" I ask.

"Yes. I really needed that. I've been feeling nothing but shit for a very long time, and this afternoon just made me see that maybe there's more to life than work. And even if I were to lose everything..." Aiden's words drop off. His smile disappears and his face falls as he ponders that possibility.

I put my hand over his hand and wait.

Aiden nods. "What I wanted to say is that even if I were to lose everything, at least I know that I have you. And that makes everything better."

I smile and wrap my arms around him. "Yes, of course. I'm here for you. No matter what."

"I love you, Ellie," Aiden whispers.

"I love you, too."

With my arms still wrapped tightly around his neck and my head on his shoulder, we remain for a few moments, enjoying the silence. I listen to the steadiness of his heartbeat and the evenness of his breaths. I no longer feel helpless. I know that just being here for him is enough for now. And I will stay here for as long as he needs me.

The rain outside intensifies and the raindrops become smaller and more powerful. They sound like little pellets hitting my window.

"I know we never really talked about it before," Aiden says after a while. "But I was wondering..."

His voice drops off. I wait for him to continue without letting him go.

"This is so dumb," he says, pulling away from me. I try to look into his eyes, but he keeps them focused on the kitchen table. It's clear that whatever he's about to ask me, he's really embarrassed about.

"What?" I nudge him. "You can ask me anything."

"I was just wondering if you would want to be...my girlfriend." Aiden looks straight into my eyes when he says that word 'girlfriend' and it hangs there in the air between us, as if it's suspended on a string.

"I know that we never talked about being exclusive. And I'm not even sure if you're interested in doing that. But I thought that I would ask...because I love you, Ellie. And I want you to be mine."

Even before any words come out of my mouth, a big smile forms on my face. I nod and wrap my arms around him as I slide into his lap. He welcomes me with both arms. He buries his fingers in my hair and gives me a big kiss.

"Is that a yes?" he asks, laughing, pulling away for a moment.

"Yes, of course, yes," I mumble through the kisses. "I thought that you would never ask."

After a few minutes of making out, I pull away. "Why were you afraid to ask me that?"

"I don't know." He shrugs. "I guess because I feel very vulnerable when I'm with you. Unlike any other woman that I've known, you actually have the ability to break my heart."

That statement sends shivers down my back.

"I haven't been exclusive with anyone since my ex-wife," he adds. "I never wanted to. Honestly, I thought that part of my life was over. I never wanted to be in a long-term exclusive relationship again. I was never really good at those things anyway. But then...you came along. And, swept me off my feet."

I shake my head.

"What? Why are you shaking your head?"

"I'm just surprised, that's all. I love you, Aiden," I whisper. "It would be an honor to call you my boyfriend."

———

AIDEN DOESN'T STAY LONG after that. He has a lot of work to get back to, trying to figure out how to salvage something that's pretty much unsalvageable; those were his words not mine.

"Oh, hey, before you go, I wanted to ask you something, too," I say. "My friend, Tom, who's engaged to my old editor at BuzzPost, Caroline Warrenhouse, has invited us to a party that her parents are having at their house in Maine. Do you want to come? My roommate, Caroline, will also probably come."

"He's marrying into the Warrenhouse family?" Aiden asks.

"Yes, you know them?"

"I've heard of them. They're quite influential. Old money. Never actually met them."

"Well, you will if you come. We can make a weekend of it," I say.

"I've never been to Maine."

"Me either. But it's supposed to be beautiful. Plus, they have this big estate on the water."

Aiden thinks about it for a moment. I'm half expecting him to decline, given everything that he's going through. But much to my own surprise, he shrugs.

"Yeah, I guess. Why not?"

"Really?"

"I've been wanting to go away with you for the weekend. And Maine sounds as good a place as any, I guess."

"Okay, great. I'll text you the details," I say, wrapping

my arms around his neck and giving him a big
wet kiss.

"You realize, of course, that Maine will be colder
than here, right?" he asks.

"Yes, I know. But I think we can brave it for a
few days."

"Only if you promise to go to the Caribbean with me
in return, sometime."

"To the Caribbean?" I ask, surprised.

"Yes."

"Of course!" I squeal. "You can take me to the
Caribbean anytime you want!"

CHAPTER 21 - ELLIE

*O*ver the next week and a half, Aiden and I don't see much of each other as he gets swamped with work and I busy myself with my self-publishing release. After participating in a few giveaways on Instafreebie and Bookfunnel, my mailing list grows to over two thousand people. I'm pleasantly surprised and terrified at the response. It's actually kind of scary to have so many people download your book. Some of the readers even wrote me really exuberant emails saying how much they have loved the story and they can't wait for the next installment.

A few days before the Maine trip, I decide that I'm ready to release the book on Amazon. I've watched some videos and have gone through some of the process of posting the book on KDP, the Kindle Direct Publishing platform. My blurb, cover, and the interior formatting is all ready since the book has already been available for free through giveaways. The thing that takes the longest is figuring out what keywords to choose. You wouldn't even believe how many podcast episodes and YouTube videos are devoted to the subject of how to choose the correct keywords.

After uploading the cover and the interior formatting, I reach the pricing stage. Since this is my first book, I decide to become exclusive with Amazon and place it into the Kindle Unlimited program. I also choose the lowest price available - ninety nine cents. After publishing, I find myself on an incredible high. No matter what happens after this, at least I have done what I've set out to do. I've published a book. And no one can take that away from me.

The book won't be available in the Amazon store for a day or two, but I decide not to waste any time and start outlining the next installment of the story. Within an hour, I have it all planned out. It's not that hard to think of what will happen next since it pretty much all happened to me before. The thing that's a bit more challenging is trying to figure out how truthful I should remain to reality. Every creative person wants to embellish and add a few details for effect. There's that expression of course, 'never let the truth get in the way of a good story.' I'm a firm believer of that. Real life is messy. People in real life don't necessarily undergo thorough transformations and have fully developed character arcs, which make for less than effective storylines. Nor are there punctuated story beats or good buildup in tension that leads to a strong climax. All essential parts of a good story. And while it's easy to just write down exactly what happened, and how it all happened, I'm not writing a memoir. I want to give a glimpse into the main character's love interest as well, and for that I need to go into his head. So, what do I do in the end? I decide to split the difference. The book is definitely inspired by my experiences on the yacht with Aiden, but it's told like a romance. Fiction. And hopefully, it will serve as a good escape for the readers.

After finishing the outline for the second book, I decide to take a break and grab a bite to eat. Unfortunately, our refrigerator is completely empty of everything edible except for condiments. Neither

Caroline nor I are very big fans of grocery shopping. I stand in front of it with the door open, staring into the plastic abyss, hoping against hope to manifest some food into existence without actually going outside.

"Want to order Thai food?" Caroline asks. Well, that's one way of doing it, I decide and nod.

After placing the order on her phone, Caroline plops down on the couch.

"This is going to be Taylor's and my first trip away," she announces.

Her eyes are lit up at the prospect of going to Maine. She was down for it as soon as I brought it up, despite the fact that she is not the biggest fan of Tom. I knew that there would be very little chance of her passing on the opportunity to meet one of the most influential families on the East Coast, but I wasn't sure if Taylor would end up coming along. I guess she has her way of convincing men to do things that they may not want to do.

"So, are you sure Taylor wants to go?" I ask.

"I'm pretty sure that he doesn't. But I promised him something nice in return."

"I don't want to know," I say immediately. I'm almost certain that it's something sexual and I already know way too much about her sex life.

"What about Aiden?"

"Actually, I think he's kind of into it," I say. "With everything that has been going on, I think he's looking forward to getting away for a bit."

Caroline knows everything that I know about Aiden's situation, which is to say not much. We watched financial news together and Aiden mentioned a few possibilities that are on the horizon. But everything is up in the air since the board of directors are planning to meet sometime soon.

"I'm honestly surprised," Caroline says. "I mean I know that he's dealing with a lot of shit right now, but I never thought of him as a particularly social person in a dinner party sort of way."

"What do you mean?" I ask, cracking a smile.

"Well, you know." She shrugs. "Going away to a party in Maine for the weekend, that your friend and his fiancée and her parents are hosting, well that's just such a boyfriend move."

I think about that for a moment. "Yeah, I guess it is a boyfriend move. But he is my boyfriend now. Officially."

Looking back now, I'm a little embarrassed about how much I gushed over the whole thing to Caroline when Aiden first asked me. But then again, despite everything, I'm kind of a romantic, and it was very sweet, kind, and loving. I love being his girlfriend.

"Of course, it couldn't hurt to go up there, right? I mean, the Warrenhouses are quite influential people. And if he were to hit it off with Mr. Warrenhouse, who knows what could happen for him in terms of bringing more investors into Owl."

"Oh, I never thought of it that way," I say, taken a little aback.

"Trust me, Aiden has," Caroline says, flipping her hair. Out of the two of us, she has always been more of a cynic, or realist, as she likes to put it.

"Perhaps, there is something that Mr. Warrenhouse could do," I say after a moment. "But I wouldn't get my hopes up. His daughter, Carrie, isn't my biggest fan. And the whole thing with Tom is rather complicated. I mean, I'm surprised that he even asked me, or even wanted me to come in the first place."

———

IT'S FRIDAY, the day of our travels to Maine. Aiden is picking me up in his car from my apartment and then we're taking a plane north. Even though I had more than enough time to pack for this trip, I, of course, have put it off to the very last moment. This morning, I grab my tattered and rather shabby carry-on bag with one broken wheel and toss in a pair of jeans, a few sweaters, and a pair of tights. I pack my makeup into a plastic bag and then pack a small amount of shampoo and conditioner and dry shampoo into a bigger plastic bag. I'm dressed in tights, boots, and a warm sweater. Maine is much colder than New York, and that's the only thing that I'm not looking forward to.

Okay, now that I'm basically packed, I also need to put together the outfit for the party. That's another thing I hate about parties on the East Coast. All the women end up dressed in mini-skirts, short strapless dresses, and open-toe shoes as if they are completely impervious to the cold and we're going clubbing in

Miami. I sigh deeply, but I don't really have any other choice. I take a short strapless red dress from my closet and a matching pair of four-inch heels. My toenails aren't in the best shape, but luckily the heels are closed-toe, providing a minimal amount of warmth.

Caroline and Taylor took an earlier flight to Bangor, Maine, so when I get the text from Aiden that he's downstairs, I make sure that I lock the apartment, otherwise it will remain open for the whole weekend. That has happened before on my watch, unfortunately. On my way out, I grab my coat as well as a hat and scarf, which I have yet to debut in New York. I always wait until it's absolutely necessary to put it on because I know that I will likely wear it for the next four months without taking a break, and that gets tedious. Even though I'm braving winter this weekend, that doesn't mean that New York will turn freezing cold quite yet, I tell myself. I might still have a week or two left of decent weather.

"You look beautiful," Aiden says when I get into his car and toss my carry-on into his backseat. Somehow, he managed to find a parking spot right in front of my building. It's so rare, and unlikely, that I almost find it sad that we have someplace to go.

"Thank you." I smile, giving him a brief peck on the lips. "You don't look too shabby either."

"Are you ready for Maine?" he asks, pulling away from the curb.

"I guess as much as I'll ever be," I joke. "No, seriously, it should be beautiful up there. I'm looking forward to that."

"And the party?"

"Um, I don't know. Parties always make me a little nervous. And I'm a little scared to see my old boss, Carrie, I won't lie."

"Well, I'll be there to soften the blow," he says.

"I appreciate that."

CHAPTER 22 - ELLIE

WHEN AIDEN TAKES ME ON HIS PLANE...

*a*iden gives the car over to the valet in front of a glass skyscraper I've never been to before. He waves to the security guard and leads me to the group of elevators in the center of the building.

We ride in the elevator, going all the way to the top of the building. I'm pretty sure we're taking a helicopter. When we reach the roof, the helicopter's propeller is already on and I can't make out anything that Aiden is saying anymore.

Aiden hands our bags over to the pilot and takes my hand. He's dressed in an impeccable blue suit without a single wrinkle in it, despite the fact that he was sitting in the car for quite some time.

His cufflinks catch the bright lights, illuminating the
roof top, blinding me for a moment with their
brightness. They have an elegant square design with
one large sparkle at each corner. I doubt that the
sparkles are anything but diamonds.

A few moments after Aiden helps me into the
helicopter, it takes off. I look out the window as the
city around us becomes nothing but a blur of model
buildings.

As we get higher and higher, I can no longer make
out the people or the cars and all the problems that
exist below seem to vanish completely.

"Where are we going?" I ask.

"To my plane," Aiden says.

"We're taking a helicopter to the airport?"

He shrugs. The corners of his mouth form a
mischievous smile. "Why not?"

I don't have a good answer. I mean, why wait in
traffic if you don't have to, right?

A few moments later, the helicopter lands on an
airstrip. It belongs to an airport that I've never been

to before. There are runways, but no large buildings for people to gather in like they have in normal, commercial airports.

Not far away, I see a plane just sitting there, waiting for us.

Aiden helps me out of the helicopter. I'm about to grab my bag, but he tells me that someone will get those for us. Holding my hand, Aiden leads me across the runway as we walk toward the plane.

The closer we get, the bigger the plane gets. It's relatively small in comparison to those large jets with three rows across on each side that I'm used to flying in.

But it's also not one of those little Cessna planes for only four or six passengers.

"Is this your plane?" I ask.

Aiden nods, leading me up the stairs of the pristine white plane with elegant lines. Inside, the plane is unlike any other one I've ever been in.

It's elegant, with luxurious leather seats. There are only a handful of them and they're big, the size of recliners. Some of the seats are facing toward the cockpit, but others are facing each other.

In the middle of the plane, the seats are even bigger, more like love seats and couches centered around a table.

"Wow," I whisper.

"You like?"

"Is this really a plane?" I ask. "It doesn't feel like a plane at all."

"A little different than flying coach, isn't it?" Aiden asks with a smile.

"I'd say."

The plane has the unique aroma of a new car smell mixed with lavender. Suddenly, a tall, gorgeous man in his mid-fifties walks up to us from the back of the plane.

He is extremely well put-together and dressed in an elegant and expensive looking suit.

"Welcome, Mr. Black. Ms. Rhodes," he says. "My name is Gordon. I will be serving you throughout the duration of the flight. Please let me know if there's anything you need."

Aiden smiles at him and asks him to bring us some water. I sit down in a large recliner seat, the size of a La-Z-Boy chair, only designed with a lot more attention to detail.

After getting us the waters, Gordon closes the door and we start taxiing down the runway.

"No announcements?" I ask.

Aiden smiles and shakes his head.

"What about all the spiel about seat belts and putting on your oxygen mask before helping the person next to you?"

"Now, why do we have to listen to that again if you're so familiar with it?" Aiden asks. I shrug and shake my head. I have no idea.

"Flying privately is a bit different," Aiden adds. "Don't worry. You'll get used to it."

"Hey, I'm already used to it."

A few moments later, Gordon comes around with

the menus. Aiden orders an Old Fashioned and I opt for a mojito.

I know that mojitos are more of a summer drink or something you order when you're on vacation in the tropics, but I've always loved their lime flavor mixed with mint.

Plus, the plane is the perfect temperature, warm and cozy, a perfect place to have a mojito.

"Your plane is...gorgeous," I say. "Thanks for taking me on it."

"Thank you for coming," Aiden says, relaxing back into his seat.

"No, thank you for coming," I say. "I mean, I know you're going through a lot and this trip may not be something that you need right now."

"Actually, I sort of think it's the exact thing I need right now," Aiden says after a moment. "Owl has been consuming my life for a long time now. And all the problems that it has been having recently...it's just nice to get away. Meet some new people. Go somewhere with a change of scenery."

Gordon comes back with our drinks.

I take a sip of mine almost immediately and savor the moment as its fresh mint flavor makes its way down the back of my throat.

I follow up that one with another one, and another one. The drink is stiff and I'm a light weight, so after only a few sips, the alcohol hits me and I feel every muscle in my body suddenly relax.

"I was talking to Caroline and she mentioned that maybe meeting the Warrenhouses might be good for you. And for Owl."

Aiden shrugs.

"Do you know them?"

"I've heard of them. Who hasn't, right? They're a pretty old family with lots of old money," he says.

"Have they ever invested in any tech?"

"I have no idea. Most tech money comes from Silicon Valley. And if they have, they would've probably done it through their various accounts and business partnerships."

"Well, maybe they'll be interested," I say hopefully.

"Perhaps." Aiden shrugs. "Though not a lot of people want to jump aboard a sinking ship."

When Gordon comes around with the menus again, Aiden orders the tomato soup made with organic tomatoes and an assortment of sushi.

I tell Gordon that I'd like the same thing. I'm not particularly hungry and sushi sounds like it would hit the spot.

We sit in silence for a bit as the airplane cruises through the air without so much as a little ripple or disturbance. I close my eyes and sink back into my seat.

This is probably the most comfortable chair I've ever sat in. It feels like it has been designed just for me. A few moments later, I open my eyes and catch Aiden staring at me.

"What?" I ask.

"You're so beautiful," he whispers.

"Thank you."

"Come here," he says after a moment. I won't lie, the last thing I want to do right now is get out of this seat, but the look on his face is...enticing. He licks his lips and motions me over to him.

My knees grow weak, but I manage to stand up and walk over. He pulls me down toward his lap.

Then he pulls my hair back and kisses me forcibly, conveying every bit of passion that I feel in his erection under me.

He's driving me wild and he knows it.

I lean over and kiss him back. I take his head in between my hands and tilt it toward me.

I bury my fingers in his thick dark locks.

I feel his hands on my back as his large cock swells underneath me.

"But what about Gordon?" I whisper through the kisses.

It suddenly occurs to me that we're not alone at all and I don't want to be walked in on in the middle of anything.

"Don't worry about him," Aiden says, pulling me closer to him. He wraps his arms around me, kissing me again.

"No, he's right out there," I say. "Okay, we can kiss, but nothing more." My words come out mumbled and slurred as I try to extricate myself a little bit from Aiden's lips without much avail.

I'm not one for public displays of affection and I don't like the idea of Gordon walking in on us doing anything inappropriate.

Despite what Aiden and I do together and no matter how much sex I put into my books, I have a firm grasp of what is appropriate or inappropriate for me to do when strangers are around.

Yet, as Aiden continues to kiss and caress my neck, I start to slowly lose myself in the moment, and I care a little bit less about Gordon, or anyone else who might walk in.

"Let me show you something," Aiden says, pulling his face away from mine.

He looks over at his seat rest and points to the button in the middle of the panel.

It's red, lit up, and has the word 'Private' on it.

"This button means that Gordon will not interrupt us until I press this button again."

"Oh, wow."

"I told you. This is my plane, and I make the rules."

Aiden moves closer to me. But instead of kissing me again, he pauses and takes off his suit jacket.

"I still feel him right over there," I say after a few moments.

"Well, in that case, we will have to do something to take your mind off him, won't we?" Aiden says with a coy smile.

He turns me around on his lap so I'm facing away from him. Then he pulls off my sweater and unclasps my bra.

My breasts fall freely into his open hands. For a moment, his hands feel cool to the touch, but refreshing at the same time.

He runs his fingers over my arms and I run my fingers up his forearms in return.

They are strong and powerful, and when he moves, there are veins that pop up in between the muscles.

Aiden kisses me along my neck, pushing me back to my feet.

He helps me out of my boots, and then he pulls down my yoga pants, leaving me just in my panties.

After he spins me around, I thread my fingers around his hair as his lips make their way down toward my nipples.

Shivers run up my spine as a warm sensation starts to build somewhere deep within me.

My fingers lose themselves in his thick hair and I only manage to tug at it lightly.

Without any more ceremony, Aiden pulls off my panties.

Now I'm standing completely nude in front of him, in the middle of his plane.

He wraps his arms around my waist and gives me a little slap on my butt.

"You have a fine piece of ass, if I may be so blunt," he says. I can't help but crack up laughing.

"Thank you, I guess."

The tone of the moment quickly grows more serious as he sits me back down on his lap, facing away from him.

He runs his fingers down my body and I lean into him. The whole world seems to fall away immediately. I'm no longer embarrassed at being naked or worried about anyone walking in on us.

Nothing else exists in this moment except for Aiden and his fingers, which are headed toward my clit.

He spreads his legs and my legs, which are on top of his, spread with his.

His fingers press on my clit and my pussy begins to throb.

I feel myself getting wet and resist the urge to pull my thighs back together.

Instead, I step my feet on top of his knees and open wide.

"Wow, baby," Aiden says, clearly impressed. "Now, this is hot." If anyone were to walk in on us right now, they'd see nothing but me spread eagle in front of them in all of my glory. But I don't care. His fingers inside of me feel too good and nothing else matters.

Aiden kisses me behind my ears as his fingers go deeper and deeper inside of me.

After a few moments of being soft and delicate, they speed up in rotation.

The faster that his fingers move, the more energy starts to build up within me.

"Oh, Aiden," I moan. I'm completely wet and my orgasm is going to be here at any moment.

"I'm getting close," I mumble.

"Yummy," Aiden says, without slowing down his efforts. I feel myself spreading open for him and I clench my toes around his knees. His fingers swirl faster and faster.

"Come for me, Ellie," he orders.

"Yes, sir," I say.

Just as those words escape my lips, I feel myself going over the edge.

The orgasm pulsates through me, making my legs go numb and shaking my whole body.

The release is so intense that I disappear completely into another world and don't come back up for air for a while.

My mind goes blank and after a few moments of

intense pleasure, my body goes completely limp. I think I would fall off his lap were it not for him holding me up.

"I love you, Ellie," Aiden whispers over and over again in my ear.

CHAPTER 23 - ELLIE

*W*e reach Bangor, Maine not long after.

We land at another private airport in pitch darkness.

The only reason I figure it's another private airport is that we get off the plane by just walking down the stairs and then head straight into the car that's waiting for us.

When we're sitting comfortably in the backseat with our luggage safely in the trunk, I give the driver the address that Tom gave me.

"Are you sure you don't want to stay at a nearby hotel?" Aiden asks. I shrug. Actually, I do, but I already promised Tom that we would stay at one of the guest cottages on the Warrenhouse property.

"It would be rude to back out now. I think they have it all ready for us."

Aiden shrugs nonchalantly. I know that no matter how he feels about it, he isn't going to press the matter any further.

An hour later, we pull up to a large gate where our driver proceeds to tell the person on the other side of the intercom who we are and what we're doing here. The gate swings open and we drive down a lush paved road surrounded on both sides by a thick forest.

"Wow, there's so much vegetation here," I say as I marvel at the trees outside.

"Welcome to Maine," Aiden says. We continue down the road for some time until the house appears in the distance. And by house, I mean, that is a big understatement. The place looks huge even from half a mile out.

"Tom said that there are at least ten bedrooms in this place," I say. "Maybe ten bathrooms, too, but that's before he lost count."

Aiden laughs. "Some people love large homes."

"You don't know?" I ask. I immediately know that it's a stupid question. I mean, I've been to his apartment and though it was definitely lavish and cost in the millions, size was not something that was particularly important to Aiden.

"I was thinking of buying a big place when Owl first started to take off, but after looking at like ten properties, I started to feel overwhelmed by them. The sheer size is just too much to take. You have to have a big staff to maintain these places, and I don't like having a ton of people around me all the time."

I nod in agreement. As much as I like the idea of owning my own apartment, I've never given the size of a house in the country much thought. Honestly, I never thought I'd ever have enough money to support a lifestyle that paid for a regular mortgage, let alone something this lavish.

As we pull up to the palatial house, I'm in awe of how big it actually is. Tom had mentioned that it was an old Queen Anne in design, sprawled over ten thousand square feet and four levels. I never knew that people back in the day would ever want a house that big, but I guess there's a first for everything. Even though it is already dark out, the house is expertly lit, making it look bigger and more spacious. Even though it is from the nineteenth century, and this is Maine, nothing about this place looks at all scary or spooky. Instead, the lighting is such that it makes it look very welcoming and charming.

The driver carries our bags as we walk up the stairs. The house has a number of gables and fish-scale shingles. The bay windows that look out onto the water out front are adorned with stained glass. Once we get to the sweeping veranda, which wraps around the ground floor of the house in both directions as far as the eyes can see, I take a moment to look out onto the blackness of the water. If tomorrow is a nice clear day, the water will undoubtedly sparkle in the sunlight. Maine is famous for its gorgeous waterways.

The driver rings the doorbell, and a few moments later, someone answers the door. I don't know who I am expecting, maybe Mrs. Warrenhouse, or at least Carrie, but Tom is the last person I expect to see.

"You made it!" he exclaims, giving me a warm hug. Once we embrace, it feels like I'm the lifeline Tom has been hoping and praying for his whole trip here.

I'm glad to be of service. After I introduce Tom to Aiden, they shake hands. While they talk about the flight over, I take a little peek inside. As much as I like old houses on the outside, I find the inside to be rather depressing. They're often too dark, especially in New England, where every speck of light should be cherished and fawned over. But much to my surprise, the interior of the Warrenhouse mansion does not have the typical dark wood floors, and even darker painted walls, well-worn rugs, and claustrophobic old drapes around the windows. Instead, everything inside is ultra-modern. Some mid-century pieces are mixed in with wonderful contemporary furniture, which gives the house life and brings it screaming into the twenty-first century.

Sensing my interest in taking a look around, Tom apologizes. "I'd love to give you a tour," he says, "but Mrs. Warrenhouse is still making final preparations for the party and she asked that all guests be shown to their cottages until tomorrow."

"I understand," I say.

"I promise, I'll give you the full tour tomorrow. It's quite...lavish."

There's a tinge of pride in Tom's intonation, mixed

with shame. I know him well enough to know that all this wealth makes him embarrassed. It always has. But at the same time, he also enjoys it. More than other people even. The thing that probably makes him shy away from it is that it's not money that he made himself. That's the conundrum, isn't it, though? He wants to be a 'serious' writer, someone who writes literary fiction that critics approve of and regular people rarely buy. So, unless he actually marries into money, like Hemingway and numerous other famous authors, there's no way he could ever live this lifestyle.

"Here, let me show you to your cottage," Tom says, walking past us down the steps. "It's just around the corner."

We follow him to the guesthouse, which is just around the corner, except that the house is so big it actually takes some time to get there. The driver insists on carrying our bags there, and I appreciate the gesture because this part of the house is poorly lit and I tend to be rather clumsy. After a few moments of walking through thick vegetation, we reach a craftsman house, which also looks like it has been built at the beginning of the century.

Though it doesn't look like much from the outside, it's quite nice on the inside. It has surprisingly tall ceilings, and it has been completely remodeled as well. With two bedrooms and two baths, a large well-equipped kitchen, and two large bay windows, it is more than enough space for the two of us.

"I love how contemporary it is on the inside," I say. "It's a nice combination of old world and new world."

"Me, too. But actually, according to Carrie, this whole style is a result of the compromise that her parents reached. Her mother loves old houses, but her father loves contemporary sleek designs. So they decided that they would buy this place and it would be remodeled and decorated to fit the times. But it still has all the history that Mrs. Warrenhouse loves."

"That sounds wonderful," Aiden comments and we both agree.

After telling us that the beds are already set up with fresh linens and there are towels for us to use in the bathroom, Tom starts to head out. I walk him outside, leaving Aiden inside.

"Thanks for...everything."

"No, thank you for coming," Tom says. "I really appreciate it."

"So, how's everything going with Carrie and her family?"

"It's fine. But you know, they're WASPs so they're a little hard to read. They like to keep their cards close to their chests."

I nod. I know exactly what he means. They are probably the type of people who would wine and dine you and treat you like a princess, but then turn on you the first opportunity they get just because being nice trumps everything including being honest.

"Well, in any case, I'm looking forward to the party tomorrow night. It sounds like it will be fun," I say.

"I hope so," Tom says, smiling. "Oh, Caroline and her date...Taylor...are here already. I'm sure that you'll see them in the morning. If you're hungry or want to get breakfast in town tomorrow, the driver will take you anywhere. I think Aiden has his number. There's nothing official going on at the house until the party."

"Got it." I nod, feeling slightly relieved. I was really

hoping that there wouldn't be any obligations for us until the party. I'm hoping to get some alone time with Aiden and really take in the scenery since I've never been here before.

"Okay, see you tomorrow night. All festivities start at six p.m."

I give him a brief hug and watch him disappear down the winding path leading to our cottage.

———

WHEN I GET BACK, Aiden has already made himself comfortable on the couch. He even started the fireplace.

"Wow, you got the fireplace going?" I ask. "So quickly?"

"It's all remote controlled." He smiles, staring at his cell phone. Walking by, I see that he's not doing work but rather reading something on his Kindle app. That's a good sign, I say to myself. But it also reminds me...

I head to my bag and retrieve my laptop. My book

should be up on Amazon by now. I check my email and spot it right away.

Congratulations! Your book is now available on Amazon.

"Oh my God!" I say, getting up from my seat and walking over to the couch with the laptop. "Here it is!"

I show Aiden my book.

"Ella Montgomery?"

"Yes, that's the pseudonym that I chose for the occasion."

"It's very pretty."

"Thanks."

"Well, let me do you the honors," Aiden says, going to his Amazon app on his phone.

"What are you doing?"

"I'm going to be your first paying customer."

"No!" I try to take his phone away, but it's too late. He's too dexterous and his arms are too long. A moment later, my book appears on his Kindle app.

"Aiden, you can't read it," I say.

"Why not?"

"Because...because, it's personal."

"It's on Amazon. A million strangers are going to be reading it."

"Well, don't you have a highfalutin view of my career as a writer? Millions? Please. I'll be lucky to get a handful."

"Even better then. So, why can't I be one of those handful?"

I shake my head. I don't really have a good answer. I'm just embarrassed over the whole thing. I mean, who am I to call myself a writer, let alone an author? I'm just some little girl with probably nothing good to say.

"Listen, Ellie. I know that you have doubts about your writing. But you really shouldn't. If it's something that you have to do, if it's your calling, who cares what anyone else thinks? Even me. Your boyfriend. And with this title and cover...I think you're bound to sell a few copies."

I take a deep breath. I won't lie. I love how

encouraging he is. His approach definitely makes me feel a little more confident than my mom's negative comments or Tom's scorn at the whole romance industry.

"Okay, but you have to promise not to freak out over all the sex that it has," I say after a moment. "I mean I know that it's a lot. But that was one of the most fun parts I had writing it."

"Oh my, how little you know me, Ellie. Of course, I won't mind the sexy bits. I love sex."

"Yes, I know you like sex," I say, rolling my eyes. "But you know, it's kind of about what happened on your yacht. So, I just don't want...things to be weird."

Even though I fancy myself a writer, I often find it difficult to use just the right words when expressing myself.

"Shh." Aiden puts his finger to his lips as he starts to read. Unable to deal with the thought of someone actually reading my book in front of me, I decide to do something useful to distract myself. I take my laptop back to the kitchen island and open my mailing list. Then I write all 2,457 people an email, asking them to post a review for the first book. I've received a number of these from other authors, so I have a vague idea of what to include. But still, I find the words difficult to come by. I re-read it a number of times before I gain enough strength within myself to actually send it. Once I do press send, I close my laptop immediately and decide to not give it any more thought tonight. Worrying about something you can't control won't change anything, so you might as well not worry. I chant this to myself over and over until I finally believe it.

An hour later, I fall asleep to an old Jewel album coming in through my earphones while Aiden is still on the couch, devouring my novel.

CHAPTER 24 - ELLIE

THE NIGHT OF THE PARTY...

The following morning and afternoon, I find myself riding a high. Aiden is quite impressed with the book and loves the sexy scenes.

He says that he has never read a book quite like it, and I tell him that if he likes it then he should check out *Fifty Shades of Grey* and some of the more popular erotic self-published authors.

Because some would say that my book is tame in comparison to theirs. Still, my heart beams with pride knowing that he approves of my writing. And not just approves.

He is actually proud of me.

He is encouraging, loving, and everything any

struggling writer full of anxieties and fueled by numerous rejections craves.

In addition to Aiden's overwhelming praise, *Auctioned Off* also drums up over thirty, four and five star reviews in a day and I receive a number of emails from people who read the free book telling me how they can't wait until the second one comes out.

I decide that if I really put my head to the grindstone and work after we get back from the weekend, I can probably have the second installment ready within the month.

By the time that I'm getting ready for the cocktail party, I even have two thousand pages read and ten sales!

"Wow, people are actually reading this book. I'm just...shocked," I tell Aiden, watching him put on another pressed immaculate suit in front of the mirror.

"Of course, they are," he says. "The blurb is awesome and so is the cover. Let alone the whole premise."

"Still, you know, lots of people have those things and don't sell anything."

"Listen, you don't have to tell me about how business works," he says, laughing.

It sounds like he's being condescending, but by the tone of his voice I know that he isn't. "When I started Owl, there were at least a handful of other programmers who had very similar ideas to mine. But Owl rose above the pack."

"How?"

"Marketing. It's all about marketing. You can have the best product out there, but if you don't have the marketing to go along with it, you're pretty much dead in the water."

I nod.

That's pretty much what all the self-publishing podcasts have also confirmed and preached. Without a good marketing strategy, it's all futile.

"But you seem to be doing the right thing. I mean, growing your mailing list. That's the key. You already have almost twenty-five hundred people who are your book's target audience and the sky's the limit. Plus, content. Content is one of the most important aspects of staying ahead. You have to keep publishing when everyone else gets tired or bored.

You need a steady flow of books to make a name for yourself."

"I know," I say, applying eyeliner to my eyes and following it up with a heavy dose of mascara.

"How long do you think you'll make this series?"

"I have no idea." I shrug.

"I'd say go with at least five books," he says. "I did some research on the genre last night after you fell asleep and you should do quite well if you have at least five in a series."

"Wow, that's a lot," I say, taken aback by how daunting that seems.

"Well, if this is what you want to do for a living, then that's what you need to do," he says.

I nod. I don't know how he knows so much about what I've been teaching myself over the last few months, but all of his advice is pretty much spot on with what everyone else has said on all those podcasts, YouTube videos, and blogs that I've devoured.

"Okay, then, well as soon as we're back, I'm going to start writing again," I say.

"There's no rest for the wicked."

Aiden turns around to face me and I'm in awe of how handsome he looks. His suit fits like a glove, accentuating every gorgeous aspect of his toned body. His shoes are polished and his hair falls slightly in his face, but that only makes him look even more handsome and polished.

"You look...amazing," he says breathlessly. I glance at myself in the mirror. Yes, he's right. I clean up well. I'm wearing my tight red dress with four inch pumps. My hair, recently washed and blow-dried, cascades around my face, softening my strong jaw. My lips are blood red to match my dress and my eye makeup is sultry, making me look just a little dangerous.

"Shall we?" Aiden gives me his arm and I follow him out of the cottage.

***

When we get to the porch of the Warrenhouses' Queen Anne estate, there are so many people coming and going that we simply walk through the grand double doors and join the party. We decide to come by at six fifteen rather than right at six, so that we're not the first people through the door. But by the time we arrive, the party is already in full swing. Everyone is dressed in their cocktail best with women in black, tight fitting dresses and high heels and men in suits that cost more than most people pay for their mortgage every month. I scan the room for a familiar face. After a few moments, I spot Tom and Carrie across the room. We make our way over, helping ourselves to glasses of wine and some hors d'oeuvres.

Tom again greets me with a warm hug and I make the introductions to Aiden. Carrie is pleasant and nonchalant as ever. She's dressed in impossibly tall heels, which accentuate the narrowness of her waist. She's a natural waif and as we speak, she towers over me. It wouldn't bother me so much if she wasn't also quite smart and witty, in addition to being gorgeous.

"So, how is everything?" I ask. I don't necessarily want to bring up BuzzPost, but it seems like it's inevitable and at least I can do it on my terms.

"Great. We're busy, as ever," Carries says. "The site's popularity is at an all-time high. So, people are loving it."

She doesn't mention the exact number of unique visitors that the site is getting, but I know that she's telling the truth. BuzzPost has always been very popular with the eighteen to twenty-four crowd.

"And how's the expansion into the world of news?" I ask.

That has always been the sticking point for them. What made them so popular initially was that they were a fluff site, a distraction, a fun place to go to get away from the world. But then they wanted to expand into real news and reporting. And as many other sites and newspapers have found out the hard way, real news with their cold hard facts isn't the most popular thing on the internet. In fact, it's quite hard to make that sort of thing interesting to keep people coming back in the middle of their workday.

"It's actually going really well. We're sending out reporters on the campaign trail to report on what's going on the ground. You know, with the presidential race coming up."

I nod.

"Tom has always been very interested in doing that sort of thing," I say to Aiden. "Right?"

"Well, yes," Tom says.

"So, are you going to be going to the battleground states?" I ask.

Tom looks away, casting his eyes toward the floor.

"You're not?" I ask. "I thought this would be the perfect opportunity for you to do what you want to do."

"Well, the department is relatively new," Carrie pipes in. "And Tom would be better served by continuing to do what he's doing in the office."

I nod, in agreement. I mean, what else is there to say, really?

"And what about you?" Carrie turns to me. "What are you up to these days?"

"I'm actually doing a lot of writing," I say. I don't really have any intention of telling her about my self-published book. The thing is that the publishing industry and people who work in it do not look upon self-publishing in the best light. It's always been something to smirk at, laugh at.

"And not just writing," Aiden says. "But also, publishing."

"Really?" Carrie asks, raising her eyebrows. "What publishing house?"

Of course, she would make this assumption. I should've had a talk with Aiden about this. But he's just too proud of my work to keep his excitement contained.

"Actually, she's publishing it herself. It's a romance," Aiden volunteers.

I want to crawl under a rock and die. I had no intentions of telling Carrie and Tom about my book any more than what I had already told him. And I definitely didn't have any intentions of telling them that I was publishing it myself.

"Oh, I see," Carrie says. "And why is that? Did you get turned down a lot?"

Yes, of course, self-publishing is the last reserve for the failed writer. At least, that's what everyone in the industry tends to think.

I take a deep breath as I consider how I should deal with this issue. The cat is out of the bag already, so there's no option of stuffing it back in.

"Well, actually no," I say. "I didn't submit it

anywhere. I've been researching the topic for some time and a lot of self-published, indie authors do quite well for themselves. Even better than those who are traditionally published. Especially, those who write romance. So, I thought I would give it a go myself. You know, make my own marketing plan, make Facebook ads, grow my mailing list, stuff like that."

"Yes, of course," Carrie says, nodding, clearly not impressed.

"I mean, I can always submit it to agents and publishers later," I add. "If things don't work out."

"Oh, c'mon, of course they will work out," Aiden says, putting his arm around my shoulder. "Your writing is brilliant and people are already loving it."

As much as I love his perfusion of praise, something about it makes me quite embarrassed in front of Tom and Carrie. Maybe it's because I know the extent of their snobbery and how little they think of self-publishing. I mean, not long ago, I was one of them. I was the one who ranted about all of these indie writers calling themselves authors and putting out a book a month. And now, I am one of them. But the thing is that that was before I knew what I was really talking about. That was before I knew anything at all about the industry and exactly how well many of these indie authors did for themselves. And even if they didn't do that well, how freeing it would be to work just for yourself and write things that you wanted to satisfy your readers.

Of course, I can't explain any of these things to Carrie. The coldness that's emanating from her is as strong as an Arctic wind. I don't really know if it's because of my quitting or because she knows a lot about what happened between Tom and I. Not that anything really happened, but he did (or does) have feelings for me and no fiancée wants to know that about the person she's about to marry. My only hope is that he had kept his mouth shut and didn't tell her anything that would hurt her feelings and not make things any better between the two of them. Because, in reality, I do actually wish them well.

Luckily for me, the conversation shifts to other topics, which are a lot less painful for me to discuss. First, we talk about how beautiful Maine is and the weather and then we turn our attention to the Warrenhouse mansion itself. Even though I've only made it through the foyer and the living room, I find myself in awe of how beautiful this house is. As soon as I mention that, an older woman who has a strong resemblance to Carrie joins our circle.

"Well, thank you very much, darling," she says, laughing and tossing her hair back. I swear she could be the spitting image of Carrie, but only ten years older.

"Ellie, Aiden, this is my mother. Eileen Warrenhouse. Mom, this is Ellie Rhodes and Aiden Black."

"It's a pleasure to meet you, Mrs. Warrenhouse," I say, extending my hand.

"Oh, please, call me Eileen," she says, waving her hand at me. "Robert! Robert! You have to come here and meet Ellie and Aiden. Aiden, aren't you the founder of Owl?"

"Yes, I am," Aiden says shyly.

"Oh my God! My husband is just going to flip! He would love to meet you."

Eileen calls her husband over again, but he's in the middle of a conversation and raises his finger to indicate that he'll be here in a minute.

"Oh, well, his loss. So, you want to know about the house?" Eileen asks, turning to me.

"Yes, very much so!"

"Well, Robert and I bought it about fifteen years ago. It was built in 1890 and it was owned by a very prominent doctor at the time, who bought it for his second wife. It was quite a scandal at the time, as you can imagine," Eileen says, finishing her glass of champagne and immediately reaching for another.

"Robert loves contemporary houses with this sleek furniture. You know, the kind that look like no one ever lives in them. I, on the other hand, love antiques. Anything with a story just gets me going. So, when we found this house, we decided to compromise. He'd let me buy this old mansion as long as I let him decorate it in his preferred style."

"A compromise is always good," Aiden says.

"You'd think that. But you're young and in love, what the hell do you know?" she says, smiling. "A compromise basically means that both parties are left unsatisfied. But you know, for the good of the marriage, this is what we agreed to do."

"Well, it turned out marvelously," I say. I have no

idea where the word 'marvelous' came from, but talking to Eileen it seemed like an appropriate thing to say.

"Robert bought this place because, despite its age, all of its internal components worked - you know like the electrical system, plumbing, water, heating and air conditioning. It had 'good bones' as he likes to say. But once we bought it, we spent a year renovating it. I didn't want to keep every part of its Queen Anne style, so we did away with the things that were just too old-fashioned and impractical and kept, or updated, the rest. Then we worked with an interior designer to choose just the right furniture so that it complemented the house and didn't cause me any migraines."

"Oh, honey, are you telling them the story of this place? Again?" Robert Warrenhouse approaches his wife and lovingly puts his arm around her shoulder.

"Of course."

"I swear, by the way she tells it, buying and renovating this place seemed to have more of an impact on her life than having a child."

Eileen stares at him and then breaks into a smile.

"Well, of course it did. It took three full years to get this place ready, and that's not counting the guesthouses. And it took only nine months to create Carrie."

We all laugh. Mr. and Mrs. Warrenhouse aren't at all as I had imagined them. I don't know why Tom has such a hard time relating to them, but to me they appear to be easy going and laid back. Very easy to talk to. Still, when my gaze goes in Tom's direction, I can sense the tenseness that's emanating from his body.

"So, you're the founder of Owl, huh?" Robert asks, turning to Aiden. "Now, that's exciting. I'd love to hear about it."

"I'm happy to share," Aiden says.

"Tell you what, let's get ourselves a couple of brandies and retire to my study. Then we can have a real chat," Robert says, putting his arm around Aiden's shoulders. Aiden nods and winks at me before following Robert out of the room.

CHAPTER 25 - ELLIE

WHEN A FRIENDSHIP IS TESTED…

Feeling a little claustrophobic and not particularly social, I take the opportunity to escape outside for some fresh air.

It's a relatively warm night for November in New England and there isn't much of a chill coming from the ocean.

I inhale the salty air and lose myself in the crispness of the moment.

"Hey," Tom says, coming out onto the porch with me. "It's a beautiful night."

I nod, rubbing my bare shoulders.

Even though it's not that cold, the night is still rather nippy, especially for someone with bare shoulders.

"Here, why don't you put on my jacket?" he says, taking it off.

I'm about to tell him no, but the moment that I feel the warmth that's emanating from it as a result of his residual body heat, I can't resist, especially, if I want to stay out on the veranda much longer.

"There are so many stars out here," I say, looking up at the sky.

Tom follows my gaze and for few minutes we stand in silence admiring the beauty of the Milky Way.

"So, Carrie's parents seem nice," I finally say.

"Yes, they are. Especially to strangers," Tom says.

"Not to you?"

"No, not exactly." He shrugs. "I mean, I don't know. They're just difficult to get along with."

I'm about to inquire as to why, but then I realize that I don't really care.

There's probably some convoluted explanation that goes all the way back to Carrie introducing Tom to them and that's just too much history to deal with on a night like this.

"Robert did seem to take a liking to Aiden," Tom remarks. I shrug and nod, continuing to stare out at the dark water ahead.

"So, I was meaning to ask you," I say, "with everything that Carrie said about BuzzPost expanding so much into real news, why aren't you going out on the campaign trail? It has always been your dream to report on politics. This seems like the perfect opportunity."

Tom shrugs and shuffles his feet from side to side.

"It's just not something that Carrie or Robert think is a good idea. I mean, they say it's not a good use of my resources. They don't think too much of beat reporters and don't really see the point of me doing it. Since there are so many more prestigious jobs to be had at the magazine."

I nod, pretending to understand.

It's a whole bunch of bullshit, and both Tom and I know it.

The problem is that he refuses to tell them what he really wants and to go after it, and no one else can do it for him but him.

But I'm not in the mood to get into this now.

"So, tell me about your book," Tom says after a few moments.

I hesitate for a moment and then tell him everything.

The cat's out of the bag.

Aiden has already told them pretty much the whole story, so there's no use in shying away from it now.

"Wow, I can't believe you're doing this. I mean, it takes a lot of guts, Ellie."

"Really?"

"Yeah. I mean to just say fuck you to traditional publishing altogether and not even bother submitting anything there. I mean, I just never knew you were so confident in your work before."

I nod.

Hmm, maybe he's right.

Maybe this does make me confident.

Or maybe arrogant or cocky are better adjectives.

Who knows?

Maybe I just don't know any better.

"You're just putting it all out there. I mean, I know that you're a good writer. But...I don't know if I could do it."

"What? Publish and market yourself?"

"Yeah, I mean, I'm not particularly outgoing and neither are you. But you're just saying 'who cares?' What will be will be."

"Well, I have a little bit more of a plan, but yeah, pretty much. I mean, I'm not going to wait around to have some editor or agent somewhere read my work and tell me it's good. I know it's good. At least, I think it's something that readers would want to read. So, I'm going to make it available for them."

While I am talking, I don't notice how close Tom has gotten to me.

He's standing barely a foot away.

In the cold air, I watch as he breathes in and out and his breaths get faster and faster.

"You're just so...amazing," Tom says, putting his hand around my shoulder.

At first, it feels like his hug is just that of an old friend. But then, it doesn't.

Tom moves some of the hair away from my neck.

Before I realize what he's doing, he leans over and presses his lips onto mine.

———

THANK you for reading Black Rules. Can't wait to read what happens to Ellie and Aiden? **One-Click BLACK BOUNDS Now!**

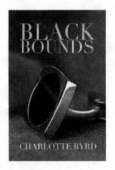

I don't belong with her.

Born into darkness, life made me a cynic incapable of love.

But then Ellie waltzed in. Innocent, optimistic, kind.

She's the opposite of what I deserve.

I bought her, but she she stole my heart.

Now my business is going up in flames.

I have only one chance to make it right.

That's where it happens...something I can never take back.

I don't cheat on her. There's no one else.

It's worse than that. Much worse.

Can we survive this?

One-click BLACK BOUNDS Now!

———

SIGN UP for my **newsletter** to find out when I have new books and stay in touch!

You can also join my Facebook group, **Charlotte Byrd's Steamy Reads**, for exclusive giveaways and sneak peaks of future books.

I appreciate you sharing my books and telling your friends about them. Reviews help readers find my books! Please leave a review on your favorite site.

BOOKS BY CHARLOTTE BYRD

ebt series (can be read in any order)

DEBT

OFFER

UNKNOWN

WEALTH

ABOUT CHARLOTTE BYRD

Charlotte Byrd is the bestselling author of many contemporary romance novels. She lives in Southern California with her husband, son, and a crazy toy Australian Shepherd. She loves books, hot weather and crystal blue waters.

Write her here:

charlotte@charlotte-byrd.com

Check out her books here:

www.charlotte-byrd.com

Connect with her here:

www.facebook.com/charlottebyrdbooks

Instagram: @charlottebyrdbooks

Twitter: @ByrdAuthor

Facebook Group: Charlotte Byrd's Steamy Reads

Newsletter

COPYRIGHT

12310763R00202

Made in the USA
Lexington, KY
20 October 2018